The Bridge in the Jungle

Books by B. Traven

THE JUNGLE NOVELS
Government
The Carreta
March to the Montería
Trozas
The Rebellion of the Hanged
The General from the Jungle

The Death Ship
The Cotton Pickers
The Treasure of the Sierra Madre
The Bridge in the Jungle
The White Rose
Stories by the Man Nobody Knows
The Night Visitor and Other Stories
The Creation of the Sun and the Moon

B. Traven

The Bridge
in the Jungle

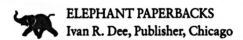
ELEPHANT PAPERBACKS
Ivan R. Dee, Publisher, Chicago

First ELEPHANT PAPERBACK edition published 1994 by Ivan R. Dee, Inc., 1332 North Halsted Street, Chicago 60622. Manufactured in the United States of America and printed on acid-free paper.

Library of Congress Cataloging-in-Publication Data:
Traven, B.
    [Brücke im Dschungel. English]
    The bridge in the jungle / B. Traven. — 1st Elephant pbk. ed.
        p.   cm.
    "Elephant paperbacks."
    ISBN: 978-1-56663-063-4

    1. Indians of North America—Mexico—Fiction. 2. Missing children—Mexico—Fiction. 3. Villages—Mexico—Fiction. I. Title.
    PT3919.T7B713 1994
    833'.912—dc20   94-25692

To the mothers
                    of every nation
                    of every people
                    of every race
                    of every color
                    of every creed
                    of all animals and birds
                    of all creatures alive
                                        on earth

The Bridge in the Jungle

1

 "Stick'm up, stranger!"

"?"

"Can't you hear, sap? Up with your fins. And you'd better snap into it!"

Through my sweat-soaked shirt I distinctly felt it was not his forefinger nor a pencil that was so firmly pressed against my ribs. It was the real thing all right. I could almost figure out its caliber—a .38, and a heavy one at that. The reason why I had been slow to obey his first order was that I believed it a hallucination. For two days while marching with my two pack mules through the dense jungle I had not met with a single human being, white, Indian, or mestizo. I knew I was still far away from the next rancheria, which I expected to reach about noon tomorrow. So who would hold me up? But it happened. From the way he spoke I knew he was no native. He fumbled at my belt this way and that; it was quite a job dragging my gun out of my holster, which was as hard and dry as wood. Finally he got it. I heard him back up. The way he moved his feet back on the ground told me that he was a rather tall fellow and either fairly well advanced in years or very tired.

"Oke, now. You can turn round if it pleases your lordship."

Fifty feet to the right of the jungle trail along which I had come, there was a little pond of fresh and not very muddy water. It had glittered through the foliage, and from the tracks of mules and horses leading to that water hole I knew that it must be a paraje where pack trains take a rest or even spend the night. So I drove my tired mules in to water them. I needed a short rest myself and a good drink.

I had not seen anyone near nor had I heard anything. Therefore I was astonished when, as if coming from a jungle ghost, the gat was pushed between my ribs.

Now I looked at him, who, as I had rightly guessed, was taller than I and slightly heavier. Fifty or fifty-five years. An old-timer, judging from the way he was dressed (which was not much different from my own get-up), cotton pants, high boots, a dirty sweat-soaked shirt, and a wide-brimmed hat of the cheap sort made in the republic.

He grinned at me. I could not help grinning back at him. We did not shake nor tell our names. Telling other people your name without being asked for it seems silly anyhow.

He told me that he was the manager of a sugar plantation about thirty miles from where we now stood, but that he preferred to manage a cocoa plantation if he only could get such a job. I told him that I was a free-lance explorer and also the president, the treasurer, and the secretary of a one-man expedition on the lookout for rare plants with a commercial value for their medicinal or industrial properties, but that I would take any job offered me on my way and that I hoped to find, maybe, gold deposits or precious stones.

"I should know about them, brother, if there were any around here. See, I'm long enough in this here part so that I know every stone and every rubber shrub and every single ebony tree you'll ever see. But then again, that goddamned beautiful jungle is so big and so rich—well, what I mean to say is, there are so many things that can bring money home to papa

2

if you only know how to use them and how to doll them up when selling them, and besides that you may actually find not only gold but even diamonds. Only don't get tired looking for them."

I felt the irony he had not put into his words but into the corners of his nearly closed eyes while speaking.

Having watered his horse, filled his water bag, and gulped down a last drink from the pond, scooped up with a battered aluminum cup, he tightened the straps of the saddle which he had loosened so that the horse might drink with more gusto, mounted his goat, and then said: "Two hundred yards from here you can pick up your gat where I'll drop it on my way. I'm no bandit. But you see, brother, what do I know about you? You might be in some kind of new racket. You seem to be green around this section of the globe. At places like the one we have had so much pleasure together—I mean this one here—a guy that's in the know doesn't take any chances, if you get what I mean. That's the reason why I relieved you of your rusty iron for a while—just to keep you from playing with it. You might have taken me for a bum after your packs and beasts and you might have slugged me just for fear of me. I know greenies like you who get dizzy in the tropics—specially if they're trailing alone through the jungle without seeing a soul or even a mole for a week. Then they see things and hear things and they talk alone to themselves and listen to the talk of ghosts. Sure, you get what I mean. In such cases the first who has his iron out is the winner, you know. I'm always happy if I can be the winner over a greeny like you. Because it's the greenies I'm ten times more afraid of than a hungry tiger. A tiger, I know what he wants if I meet him, and maybe I can trick him, but a greeny who has been three days alone on a jungle trail, you never know what he might do when he sees you suddenly standing before him. Well, so long, brother, and good luck in discovering a new kind of rubber shrub."

I went after him and I saw him drop my gun. This done, he

3

spurred his horse and two seconds later the jungle had swallowed him.

When I found myself once more alone with my mules, a strange sensation came over me that I had dreamed the whole intermission. I tried to think it all through and then I knew that every word I had heard him say, whether in my imagination or in reality, was a true statement of facts. You can easily fall victim to any sort of hallucination when you're traveling alone through the jungle, if you're not used to it. I decided to be on my guard against the jungle madness he had talked about. I also decided that the next time I met someone in the jungle I would do my best to be the winner—by doing exactly what that man had done to me.

Three months later, in an entirely different region, I was riding across the muddy plaza of an Indian village when I saw a white man standing in the portico of a palm-roofed adobe house.

"Hi, you! Hello!" he hollered at me.

"Hello yourself!"

It was Sleigh.

He invited me into his house to be introduced to his family. His wife was Indian, a very pretty woman, with a soft, cream-like, yellowish skin, brown eyes, and strong, beautiful teeth. He had three kids, all boys, who easily could pass as American boys from the South. His wife was at least twenty-five years younger than he. The oldest of the kids was perhaps eight years old, the youngest three.

His wife fried me six eggs, which I ate with tortillas and baked beans. For drink I had coffee, cooked Indian fashion, with unrefined brown sugar.

On my entering the house his wife had greeted me: "Buenas tardes, señor!" accompanied by an almost unnoticeable nod of her head, which wore a crown of two thick black braids.

4

After this short salutation, nearer to suspicion than to friendliness, I did not see her again. Neither did the children come in again, although I heard them playing and yelling outside.

The house was as poor as could be. There was practically no furniture, save one cot, a crude table, three crude chairs, and a hammock. Besides these things there were two trunks in the room, old-fashioned and besprinkled with mud. The house had two doors, one in front, the other at the back leading to a muddy and untidy yard. Yet there were no windows. The floor was of dried mud.

Sleigh, whose first name I never learned, did not invite me to stay overnight. It was not that he was ashamed that he could not offer me a bed; it was simply in accordance with a rule that a man traveling by horse or mule over the country knows best when to stay overnight and where, and therefore he is not urged to change his plans. If on the other hand the traveler were to ask whether he might stay overnight, he is sure to meet with unrestricted hospitality.

I did not ask Sleigh what he was doing here and how he made his living, nor did he by word or gesture indicate that he was curious to know what sort of business brought me through that little native village so far out of the way of regular communications.

2

 One year later I was making a rather difficult trip on horseback on the way to the jungle sections of the Huayalexco River, where I hoped to get alligators, the hides of which brought a very good price at that time. My task turned out to be far tougher than I had expected.

At certain places along the river-banks the jungle was so dense that it would have taken many days of hard work with the help of natives to clear the banks sufficiently to enable me to approach the points where alligators were supposed to be found. Other parts of the region were so swampy no one could pass them to reach the banks. I then decided to ride farther down the river, expecting to locate territory easier to hunt in. Indians had told me that on my way downstream I would meet with a number of tributaries which at that time of the year were likely to abound with alligators.

One day while on this trip down the river I came to a pump-station practically hidden in the jungle. This pump-station was railroad property. It pumped the water from the river to another station many miles away, from where it was pumped on to the next railroad depot. For about a hundred miles along the railroad there was no water all the year round save during a couple of months when the rainy season was at its height. Hence the need to pump water to that depot. Part of this water served the engine. The greater part, though, was carried by train in special tanks to the various other depots and settlements along the railroad track, because all the people living there would have left the depots and the little villages if they were not provided with water during the dry season.

The pump-master, or, as he liked to be called, el maestro maquinista, was Indian. He worked with the assistance of an Indian boy, his ayudante. The boiler was fired with wood, some of it brought in from the jungle by an Indian woodchopper on the back of a burro, the rest carried, in the form of old, discarded timber and rotten sleepers, from the depot.

The boiler looked as if it were ready to burst any minute. The pump, which looked as though it had been in use for more than a hundred years, could be heard two miles away. It shrieked, howled, whistled, spat, gurgled, and rattled at every nut, bolt, and joint—and the first day I was there I stayed a safe distance away in the fear that this overworked and mistreated dumb slave might throw off its chains and make a dash for freedom. The railroad, however, was justified in using this old pump until it broke down for good. To dismantle it, take it to the depot, and ship it to a junk yard would have cost more than half the price of a new pump. So it was cheaper to keep it where it was and let it work itself to death. Owing to the difficulties of transportation and mounting, it would have been bad economy for the railroad to bring down a new pump at this time, especially since the railroad expected that any day now an American company would strike oil near by and that this company would then take care of the water problem for a hundred miles along the track.

About seventy yards from the pump a bridge crossed the

7

river. This bridge, built and owned by the oil company and made of crude heavy timber, was wide enough so that trucks could pass over it, but it had no railings. The oil company had considered railings an unnecessary expense. Had there been railings on the bridge, perhaps this story would never have been told.

"We have lots of alligators in that river, montones de lagartos, señor, of this you may be assured," the pump-master said to me. "Of course, you will understand, mister, they are not right here where the pump is."

I could understand this very well. No decent alligator who respects established morals would ever be able to live near that noisy pump and keep fit to face life's arrows bravely.

"You see, mister, I wouldn't like them around here, never. They would steal my pigs and chickens. And what do you think, and you may not believe it, but it's true just the same, they even steal little children if they're left alone for a while. No, around here there are very few if any and these are only very small ones, too young to waste a bullet on. Farther down and also upstream, three or four miles from here, you will find them in herds by the hundred—and bulls, dear me, I think they must be three hundred years of age, so big they are."

I nodded towards the opposite bank. "Who lives over there? I mean right there where the huts are."

"Oh, there, you mean. There is prairie, mucha pastura. In fact, it's sort of a cattle ranch. Not fenced in. All open. It belongs to an Americano. After you pass that prairie there's thick jungle again. If you ride still farther through that jungle about six or eight miles, you'll find an oil camp. Men are drilling there, testing holes to see if they can find oil. So far they haven't, and if you ask me, I think they never will. That's the same people what have built this bridge. You know, if they want to drill for oil they have to get all the machinery down here from the depot. Without a bridge they couldn't pass the

8

river with such heavy loads. They tried it a few times during the dry season, but the trucks got stuck and it took them a week to get them out again. The bridge has cost them a lot of money, because the timber had to be brought fifteen hundred miles, and, believe me, mister, that cost money."

"Who lives on that ranch over there?"

"A gringo, like you."

"That's what you told me before. I mean who looks after the cattle?"

"Didn't I tell you right now? A gringo."

"Where does he live?"

"Right behind that brush."

I crossed the bridge on my horse, pulling my pack mule along behind me.

Behind a thick wall of tropical shrubs and trees I found about ten of the usual Indian chozas or jacales—that is, palm-roofed huts.

Women squatting on the bare ground, smoking thick cigars, and bronze-brown children, most of them naked, a few dressed in a shirt or ragged pair of pants, were everywhere. None of the little girls, however, was naked, although only scantily covered by flimsy frocks.

From here I could see across the pasture which the pump-master had called the prairie. It was about a mile long and three-quarters of a mile wide. On all sides it was hemmed in by the jungle. The tracks where the oil company's trucks had passed over the prairie were still visible.

It was quite natural to find an Indian settlement here. The pasture was good and there was water all the year round. The Indians need no more. The pasture was not theirs, but that didn't bother them. Every family owned two or three goats, two or three lean pigs, one or two burros, and a dozen chickens, and the river provided them with fish and crabs.

The men used to cultivate the land near their huts, raising

corn, beans, and chile. But since the oil company had started to exploit its leases, acquired twenty years before, many of the men had found work in the camps, from which they came home every Saturday afternoon, remaining until early Monday morning. The men who did not like the jobs, or who could not get them, made charcoal in the bush, which they put into old sacks to be transported by burro to the depot, where it was sold to the agents who came once a week to every depot on the railroad line.

Neither the women I saw nor the children paid any attention to me as I passed them. During the last two years they had become used to foreigners, because whoever went to the oil camps by truck, car, or on horseback stopped at this settlement, or at the pump-station, even if only for an hour or two, but frequently for the night if they arrived at the bridge late in the afternoon. Everyone, even the toughest truck-drivers, avoided the road through the jungle at night.

Among the huts I noted one which, although built Indian fashion, was higher and larger than the rest. It was located at the end of the settlement, and behind it there was a crudely built corral. No other hut as far as I could see had a similar corral.

So I rode up to that hut which boasted a corral and, obeying the customs of the land, halted my horse respectfully about twenty yards away to wait until one of the inhabitants would notice my presence.

Like all the other jacales, it had no door—only an opening against which, at night, a sort of network of twigs and sticks was set from the inside and tied to the posts. The walls were made of sticks tied together with strips of bast and lianas. Therefore if a visitor didn't wait some distance from the house until he was invited in he might find the inhabitants in very embarrassing situations.

I had waited only a minute before an Indian woman ap-

10

peared. She looked me over, said: "Buenas tardes, señor!" and then: "Pase, señor, this humble house is yours."

I dismounted, tied horse and mule to a tree, and entered the hut. I found the Indian woman who had greeted me to be the wife of my old acquaintance Sleigh. After recognizing me she repeated her greeting more cordially. I had to sit down in a creaking old wicker chair which was obviously the pride of the house. She told me that her husband would be here any minute now. He was out on the prairie trying to catch a young steer which had to be doctored because it had been gored by an older bull and now had festering wounds.

It was not long before I heard Sleigh ordering a boy to open the gate of the corral and drive the steer in.

He came in. Without showing even the slightest surprise he shook hands with me and then dropped into a very low, crude chair.

"Haven't you got a paper with you? Damn if I've read or seen any paper for eight months, and believe me, man, I'd like to know what's going on outside."

"I've got the San Antonio *Express* with me. Sweat-soaked and crumpled. It's five weeks old."

"Five weeks? Hombre, then I call it still hot from the press. Hand it over!"

He asked his wife for his spectacles, which she pulled out of the palm leaves of the roof. He put them on in a slow, almost ceremonious manner. While he was fixing them carefully upon his ears he said: "Aurelia, get the caballero something to eat, he is hungry."

Of each page he read two lines. He then nodded as if he wished to approve what had been said in the paper. Now he folded it contemplatively as if he were still digesting the lines he had read, took off his specs, stood up, put the glasses again somewhere between the palm leaves under the roof, and finally pushed the folded paper behind a stick pressed against the

11

wall, without saying thanks. He returned to his seat, folded his hands, and said: "Damn it, it's a real treat to read a paper again and to know what is going on in the world."

His desire for a newspaper had been fully satisfied just by looking at one, so that he could rest assured that the people back home were still printing them. Suppose he had read that half of the United States and all of Canada had disappeared from the surface of the earth, I am sure he would have said: "Gosh, now what do you make of that? I didn't feel anything here. Anyway, things like that do happen sometimes, don't they?" Most likely he would not have shown any sign of surprise. He was that kind of an individual.

"I'm here to get alligators."

"After alligators, you said? Great. There are thousands here. I wish you'd get them all. I can't get them away from my calves and my young steers. They make so damn much trouble. What's worse, the old man blames me. He tells the whole world that I'm selling his young cows and pocketing all the money, while in fact the alligators get them and the tigers and the lions, of which the jungle is packed full. I can tell you, the old man that owns this property, he is a mean one. How can I sell a cow, even a very young one, or anything else, without everybody here knowing about it. Tell me that. But he is so mean, the old man is, and so dirty in his soul, that's what he is. If I wasn't here looking out for his property, I can swear he wouldn't have a single cow left. But he himself is afraid to live here in the wilderness, because he is yellow, that's what he is."

"He must have money."

"Money, my eye. Who says money? I mean he hasn't much cash. It's all landed property and livestock. Only, you know, the trouble is there is nothing safe here any longer, no property, and cattle still less so. It's all on account of those bum agraristas, you know. Anyhow, I absolutely agree with

12

you that you can easily shoot a hundred alligators here. Whole herds you can shoot if you go after them. There are old bulls among them that are stronger than the heaviest steer, and they are tough guys too, those giant alligator bulls. If one of them gets you, man, there isn't anything left of you to tell the tale. But, come to think of it, why don't we first go after a tasty antelope?"

"Are there many antelope here too?" I asked.

"Many isn't the right word, if you ask an old-timer. You just go into the bush over there. After walking say three hundred feet, you just take down your gun and shoot straight ahead of you. Then you walk again a hundred feet or so in the same direction and there you'll find your antelope stone dead on the ground, and more often than not you'll find two just waiting to be carried away. That's how it is here. I'll tell you what we can do. Stay here with me for a few days. Your alligators, down the river or up it, won't run away. They will wait with pleasure a few days longer for you to come along and get them. What day is it today? Thursday. Fine. You couldn't have selected a better day. My woman will be off tomorrow with the kids for a visit to her folks. I'll take them to the depot. Day after I'll be back again. From that day on we'll be all by ourselves here, and we can do and live as we like. The whole outfit and all the house will be ours. One of the girls of the neighborhood will come over and do all the cooking and the housekeeping."

3

On Saturday morning Sleigh returned. In the meantime I had been fishing, with not much result.

"Tonight there will be a dance," Sleigh said. "The party is to be on the other side of the river, on that square by the pump. It's the pump-master who has ordered music."

"Out of his own pocket?"

"Of course. You see, it's this way: he has also ordered two cases of bottled beer and four cases of soda and lemonade from the general store at the depot. That's how he will get his money back for the music."

"How many musicians?"

"One fiddler and one with a guitar."

"That music can't cost much."

"Certainly not. But he won't get rich on the beer and soda either. He'll make a little profit all right, which he deserves since he takes the risk of bringing the music out here."

The Indian girl Sleigh had talked about had come already and was busy about the house. Although she was hardly out of her baby shirt herself, she had with her a baby of her own.

"The guy she got the brat from has left her," Sleigh said.

She was not a pretty girl; in fact, she was ugly.

"It seems to me," I said, "that man saw her only at night or when he was drunk, so when he saw her for the first time by daylight or after he had sobered up, he got so sick that he couldn't help but run as far as his feet would carry him. Somehow, I think that girl should be grateful to the night when it happened. Without that dark night she might never have had a baby. Now, since she has one, it's not unlikely that another guy might get interested in her, believing her possessed of rare qualities which can't be seen from the outside."

Sleigh eyed me for a while with a quizzical look, as if he had to think out what I had just said. When he got the point or at least thought that he had caught up with it, he nodded and said: "There is something in what you say. She certainly has had her fun. And if you ask me I am sure she is not a bit sad about it that this guy left her. It isn't that. It is only that she can't have the same fun every night that worries her."

We sat down and ate tortillas and frijoles while the girl was baking the few fish I had caught early that morning. She just laid them upon the open fire and all she did was to watch that they didn't get burned.

The hearth was a simple affair. It consisted of an old wooden box, three feet by two, which had been filled with earth and put on four sticks.

In the afternoon I rode with Sleigh over the prairie to look at the cattle. We also searched for fresh tracks of antelope. As I had expected, there were no such tracks.

"They must have migrated," Sleigh said. "They sometimes do and then you can't possibly find any tracks."

Early in the evening when we were eating dinner I asked Sleigh whether only the people who lived in this settlement would be at the dance. He explained that at least eighty, even a hundred, other people would join the party. They would

15

come from all directions, from settlements, hamlets, and huts hidden deep in the jungle, and they would come from little places along the river-banks and from ponds and creeks in the bush. Many would travel from five to eight miles on horseback, on mules or burros; some would come from even farther away.

"How does the pump-master advertise this party?"

"No difficulty at all," Sleigh said. "Whichever native comes this way is told that on this Saturday or that there will be a dance at the pump-station, and that music has been ordered already. So every passer-by takes the word wherever he goes and the people who receive the word repeat it to their neighbors and friends and whoever comes their way. It's remarkable, I tell you, how quickly such a notice reaches twenty miles in every direction."

4

 Night had fallen and we were on our way to the
pump-station on the other side of the river.
While passing Sleigh's neighbors, I observed that one hut
had a lantern tied by string to a post in its portico. When I
came closer I saw an Indian sitting on a bench and playing a
fiddle. He seemed to be about forty-five years old. A few silky
black hairs, so few that one could easily count them, framed
his brown chin. I was sure that because of these few hairs his
friends called him the one with a beard. He played pitifully
badly, but he tried hard and with some success to keep time.

"What's that?" I asked Sleigh. "I thought you said the dance
would be at the pump-station."

"Sure enough. Well, the fact is I don't know. Anyway, I
don't think the dance will be here."

"Then why should these people here have cleaned up the
whole front yard? And here's this elegant lantern. They don't
look to me so fat that they'd use lanterns just for the fun of
it."

"In a minute we'll know all about it. The pump-master will

tell us. Anyway, why shouldn't they have their own dance if they want to? There are always two or three parties going on around here. Perhaps he has had a row with the pump-master and wants to have his own party."

We had reached the opposite bank. On one post of the portico of the pump-master's hut there also was a lantern hung up. The light it gave was less bright than the one we had just seen at the fiddler's. This lantern was smoking and the glass was not cleaned. But the square in front of the pump-master's hut was well swept.

Six Indian girls who were constantly giggling about nothing in particular tried to sit on a rough bench which wasn't long enough for three. They were already made up for the dance. Their beautiful thick black hair was carefully combed and brushed. They wore it hanging down their backs, reaching almost to their hips. On their heads, fastened to their hair, they had crowns made of fiery red wild flowers. Their brightly colored muslin dresses were clean and neatly ironed. A heavy odor of cheap, strongly perfumed soap surrounded them. When they saw us coming, they stuck their heads together, hid their faces behind their shawls, and chatted and giggled even more than before, as if every one of them knew a good story about Sleigh or me.

The pump-master was leaning against the post from which the lantern was hanging.

"Now, what's the matter?" Sleigh asked. "Do we get a dance or do we? If not, say so, and I'll turn in."

The pump-master scratched his head, coughed and spat several times before he said: "I wish I knew myself. First thing, to tell you the naked truth, the orchestra hasn't come yet. Frankly speaking, I don't think they'll come at all. It's too dark now. They are afraid to ride through the jungle after dark. I don't blame 'em. Por Jesu Cristo, I'm afraid myself to ride through that goddamned jungle at night, and I know every trail and every vereda for twenty miles around. These

18

two guys promised by all the saints that they would be here by five in the afternoon. I'm sure they've been caged by another party right at the depot and have been promised better pay. So these lazy sticks said to themselves: 'Why should we ride through that nasty jungle for hours and under that blazing sun if we can stay right here at the depot and get more money?' You would do the same, mister, or would you?"

"Since you ask me, Don Agustín, I don't care and I can't even play *Dixie* on a comb, still less a mouth-organ. Christ, I'm tired and I'd like to turn in." Sleigh yawned as wide as his mouth would permit.

"Have a cigarette." The pump-master offered Sleigh the little tobacco bag. Sleigh pulled out a corn leaf, shaped it, pressed it between his thumb and forefinger, poured the black tobacco on it, wetted it, and began to roll it.

"You wouldn't like our cigarettes," the pump-master said to me while helping himself. "Take one of these here, they'll suit your taste better. You gringos prefer to be fooled about real tobacco." He pulled out of his other shirt pocket one of our most advertised brands imported from back home. "I never smoke that sissy stuff," he said, "I only carry them for the oil people who come this way to make them feel at home and sell them a few bottles of beer."

"What's going on at Garcia's over there?" Sleigh asked. "Is he throwing a competition party or doing a dance all his own?"

"Perhaps he is. How should I know? The fact is, his big boy, his oldest son, I mean, has come home for the week-end. He came all the way down from Texas, where he works in the oil fields somewhere between San Antonio and Corpus Christi, as he tells me, and he is making good money too. He looks like a prince, the boy does. So maybe the old man is celebrating that event. He is always on the spring for an occasion to show what he can do on the fiddle."

After this talk, seeing that the party seemed far off, we

19

returned to Sleigh's place. He was, as he told me on our way back to the other bank, concerned about a certain cow that hadn't come home yet.

Garcia was still sitting in the portico of his jacalito, whimpering on his violin and putting all his soul into it.

This time I saw the big boy from Texas sitting beside his father. He was about twenty, for an Indian rather tall, clean and carefully combed. From the creases that were still in it I could see that the shirt he wore was brand-new. In a way his attitude was that of a rich uncle paying a visit to poor relatives. His face showed clearly how happy he felt to be the spoiled member of his family. On his left knee he held an enameled cup full of black coffee, as I learned a minute later when part of it was spilled over the ground. On his right knee he rested his elbow and in his right hand he held an enchilada —that is, a tortilla filled with cheese, onions, chicken, and chile. From long experience he had learned how to eat without moving his arms and hands more than absolutely necessary. Had it not been for his laughter and his happy face, one might have thought that an automaton and not a human being was having supper. He was preparing himself for a ten-hour dance, so he tried his best to avoid any waste of man-power. He would not worry whether the music arrived or not. As long as there was a fiddle around and a few good-looking girls, there was sure to be a party also.

At the very moment when we were just in front of Garcia's, the loud and over-excited voice of a child could be heard: "Ay, alloh, Manuelito, what's the trouble with you? Still not ready?" And as if he had been shot from a catapult a little boy sprang from behind the hut into the portico. With the agility of a young leopard he jumped straight upon the neck of his big brother, so that coffee and enchilada, or what was still left of them, tumbled over onto the sand.

Once the little boy was firmly settled on his brother's neck, he began savagely mussing the hair that had been so carefully oiled and combed for the dance. When the hair looked like that of an enraged madman, the little boy's fists started hammering the neck, the head, and the shoulders of his brother so furiously that the poor victim of that terrific onslaught finally had to stand up. With heavy, good-natured laughter he tried to shake off the little cat riding on his neck. Carlosito, the little brother, now no longer able to hold on, glided down his brother's back. Hardly had he reached the ground when he took a boxer's position before his brother and challenged him to a fight. Manuelito accepted, saying that he would teach the little one how a real prize-fighter boxes.

Carlosito, however, was not fully himself. Accustomed to stand, walk, and run barefooted since he was born, he now felt unsure on his feet. He had the feeling that his feet were clamped to the ground when he tried to lift them and that they were wrapped in iron so tightly that they could get no air. All the flexibility and lightness of his feet, which heretofore had made him feel like a young antelope, he had suddenly lost without knowing why. So when he tried to fight, his little body swayed and wriggled.

Manuel had brought along with him, as a present for his kid brother, a pair of genuine American shoes. The soles of these shoes were polished and they were smooth as glass. Carlosito, of course, had to put on his new shoes to show the giver how much he liked them. Never before in his life had he worn shoes on his feet. So it was only natural that he should feel the way he did about the heaviness and insecurity of his little feet.

Garcia scratched his fiddle untiringly, not in the least bothered or molested by the noise.

"The kid is pitch crazy about his big brother," Sleigh said to me while we were walking to his place. "It's funny how things are in this world. These two boys are only half-brothers. The big one and another about fifteen years old are the ones Garcia had by his first wife. The second, the one who is fifteen, is not quite right in his mind. At least that's what everybody here, me included, thinks. He has the craziest ideas and he does the most stupid things. The little one Garcia had by his second wife, the one he is living with now. She is very young, more than twenty years younger than he. Yet they seem to be very happy, never have a row. Manuel, the big boy, has come here for no other reason than to see his kid brother, who is as mad about him as the big one is about the kid. He has spent practically all his savings just to make this trip to bring the kid a pair of new shoes and a little ukulele. The trip alone takes more time than he can spend here. The second one—I mean the one who's half-witted—is absolutely indifferent about his two brothers and about his father and his stepmother too. Often I get the idea that he is jealous of the kid, I don't know why, and that he's waiting for a chance to do the kid some harm. He has already played many nasty tricks on him—burning his feet when the kid was asleep, or pulling out a tuft of his hair, or throwing snakes at him, or putting ticks all over him. That's one of the reasons why we all think him screwy."

We had arrived at Sleigh's hut. In one corner of the large room, the only room the hut possessed, the girl had arranged her bedding on the earthen floor. It consisted of a petate, a sort of bast mat. An old blanket full of holes—her cover—lay on the mat. Over this simple bed a mosquito bar was hung.

Hardly had we entered when Sleigh again left to see if the missing cow had come home.

The girl, not minding my presence at all, squatted on the floor, pulled down her dress almost to her hips, and let her baby drink. As soon as the baby was satisfied, she pulled her dress up again and, holding her baby in one arm, crawled beneath the mosquito bar. From the movement of the netting I judged that she was undressing. Then I heard her stretch out her limbs while she uttered a long sigh, by which she obviously meant: "Well, folks, I think I deserve my rest, so leave me alone." The fact was that the work she had done during the day had been so easy that a child could have accomplished it. To her it meant nothing whether the world outside her mosquito bar was heading for a gay night with music and dancing or for a tragedy. She had her baby, her eats, and a dry place to sleep in. That was all she wanted on earth.

5

 It was dreary in the hut. The little lamp—a tin container filled with kerosene, with a strip of wool stuck in it for a wick—smoked and gave only a spark of light, which made this gloomy, primitive room seem ghostly—a place that gave you no hint that there was civilization somewhere in the world. Any minute I expected to see phantoms of dead Indians and strange animals appear. Everywhere in the hut there were little shadows dancing about, as the smoking flame fluttered in the soft breeze that came in through the walls. I thought I saw big spiders, tarantulas, and huge black scorpions crawling along the wooden rafters on which the palm roof rested.

Frequently the flame got so low that through the walls I could see the flicker of lights in the near-by jacales. The knowledge that there were other huts inhabited by people close by did not make me feel easier in the least. I did not know these people. They all were Indians and if, superstitious as they were, they thought I might bring them or their children harm, they would sneak in and kill me, then throw me into the river; and before Sleigh returned, every trace of what had happened would have been washed away.

Beetles, moths, mosquitoes, and night butterflies bigger than my hands entered the open door. Flying around the little lamp, they deepened the ghostliness of the room rather than brought life into it.

Now and then a gurgling or a gulping sound would come from the river, whose bank was less than twenty yards away. Not only the air around me, but also the ground seemed to be filled with a never tiring sobbing, whistling, whining, hissing, fizzing, whimpering. A burro brayed plaintively in the prairie. A few others answered him, as if they wished to encourage him against the dangers of night. Then a cow mooed. A mule came running close to the open door, chased by a real or perhaps an imagined enemy. On looking into the hut and seeing a human being sitting quietly inside, it recovered from its fear or dream or whatever it was, sniffed at the earth, then calmly walked back to the pasture.

Now and then I heard fragments of speech and hushed voices. A shrill laugh cut the night, reached me, and vanished at the same moment. From another direction came a woman's yell. For a second her yell hung in mid-air, then fell to the ground and was swallowed by the whining jungle. It left behind it a deeper night, a more intense gloom. A few trembling notes from a fiddle floated on the breeze. They came as if they were dancing through the night, but before they actually came close to me they were adrift again.

And there, suddenly, like a shadow, Sleigh stands in the entrance to the hut. All I can see of this shadow is the face. His sudden, silent appearance makes me gasp. I am glad in a way that he cannot see my face at this moment.

"Hell, I wonder if that lazy piece of a girl has left me a gulp of coffee." His words give me back my breath. "The devil, I am thirsty."

The girl, that lazy piece, knows no English, but coffee she has understood and from the questioning tone in his voice she knew what Sleigh wanted.

So from under the mosquito bar she says: "There is some left on the fire on the hearth." Of course, she answers in Spanish.

While Sleigh was away she had slept profoundly, as I gathered from her deep, quiet breathing. Nevertheless, with the excellent hearing of an Indian, she had been aware of Sleigh's coming, while I, fully awake and facing the entrance, had heard nothing.

"De veras?" Sleigh says. "That's almost as good as a diamond found on the prairie." In a tired manner he goes to the back of the hut where the enameled pot full of coffee had been left on the smoldering ashes of the hearth.

"How about you, Gales? Have 'nother cup of coffee?"

"No. Thanks just the same."

The girl snores already. As quickly as she had come out of her dreams, so quickly had she returned to them.

Sleigh sat before me. After a time during which he seemed to doze he said: "Damn the whole outfit. I can't find that devil of a cow. Not for a thousand dollars could I bring her home. She has got her calf here in the corral, that damn devil has. Every evening she comes home all right without any trouble. Also at mid-day when it gets too hot and the cattle are plagued by horseflies, she comes in with all the others to lie down under the trees. I'm plumb sure we've got a lion around. Maybe even a couple of lions. Perez, one of the neighbors, he has a fine goat, a milker, she hasn't come home for days. He too is sure we've got lions. The fact is that goat will never come home again. It's gone for good. The cow has always been very punctual, almost like a clock. Something is queer about the whole damn machinery, that's what I tell you. Well, we'll see tomorrow. Now, in such pitch-dark night, I can do nothing about it, not a thing."

26

A minute later he's asleep. In spite of his being asleep he nods, frowns, murmurs, smiles at what I say, just as if he were awake.

"Hi, you!" I shout suddenly. "Listen, you, if you wish to sleep, all right, then, sleep, only don't let me talk here to the walls."

"Asleep? Who is asleep? I asleep?" he yells as if I had insulted him. "I'm never asleep. I don't sleep at all. That's just the trouble here. I haven't got no time to sleep. I've heard every word you said. That thief Barreiro you are talking about. Gee, I've known him for years. Didn't I know him when I was on that cocoa plantation down near Coacoyular? He's a thief all right, and a killer too, if you ask me."

"What's the matter with that dance?" I ask him. "The whole day long we've heard nothing else but the dance tonight. Is there a dance or is there? If not, well, I'll turn in. I'm sick of that babble about a dance which never happens."

"All right, all right, don't get upset about that dance. Here we take our time and don't hustle. Let's go once more to the pump and see how things are. I'm sure the pump-master has got the problem solved. He doesn't want to be stuck with his beer and his soda."

Without hurrying, Sleigh pulled down his leather pants, looked around until he found a broken comb, combed his hair as butchers and saloon-keepers used to wear it twenty-five years ago, put on a pair of yellow cotton pants, and then said: "Well, I'm all set now for the dance. Let's go. If I only had the faintest idea where that damned cow might be!"

When we passed Garcia's home I noticed that the lantern was still hanging on the post in the portico. Garcia, though, was no longer sitting on the bench. Nor did I see the two boys. Through the wall I got a peep at Garcia's wife, making up by the dim light of a lamp like Sleigh's.

"Well, well!" I said to him. "There will be a dance all right. The señora is putting on her very best for the great event."

27

6

 The night is thick with blackness. None of the stars that are so bright in the tropics is visible.

At the river-bank we have to feel our way to the bridge. From the opposite bank the pump-master's lantern gave us a vague indication of our way. After some groping, more with our feet than with our hands, we finally hit the heavy planks.

"Christ!" I suddenly yelled. "That surely was a narrow escape from a bath in the river. Seems to me, one has to be as careful here as if walking a tightrope. Only an inch to the left and I would have toppled off that damn bridge."

Sleigh showed no excitement about my adventure. He only grumbled passionlessly: "Yes and God knows you have to be extremely careful at night trying to make the bridge. If you're drunk you have no chance. There is no rail you know."

"How deep do you think the river might be here near the bridge?"

"Between eight and fifteen feet. The banks are low. On the average I should say it is eight feet deep. Right in the middle of the stream, if you want to call that lazy current a stream, it is about fifteen feet."

28

"Deep enough to disappear forever," I said, "and even suppose you are a good swimmer, if it is as pitch dark as it is tonight, you can swim around in a circle without realizing it and never reach either bank."

Talking to Sleigh and thus not paying much attention to how I was walking, I had marched straight ahead, when all at once I saw right beneath the tips of my boots another light. This surprised me so much that I halted with a jerk to examine that great marvel of a light in the water. However, my surprise was shortlived, for I quickly realized that the light in the water was but the reflection of the pump-master's lantern. My right foot had struck the rim, which was about six inches wide and six inches high—just high enough to prevent a truck from gliding off the bridge when the planks were covered by slimy mud during the rainy season. Had I walked a bit faster I would undoubtedly have lost my balance on striking the rim and I would have tumbled over and into the river.

On reaching the end of the bridge we found several Indian youngsters sitting on the planks. They were singing Mexican songs, and also American ones translated into Spanish. Their legs dangled over the edge, swinging in time to the tunes they sang. Mostly they stayed within a range of only seven notes. Yet presently and without warning their voices jumped up two full octaves. As they could not sing notes that high, they shrilled them at the top of their voices. Anywhere else under heaven such singing would have sounded insane. But here in a warm tropical night, surrounded by a black and forever threatening jungle, noisy with thousands and thousands of voices, whispers, melodies, and tunes blended with the gentle sound of the river, their singing seemed proper and in harmony with the whole universe.

To the left of the bridge was the pump-station. To the right was a wide, open sandy space, with very coarse grass trampled down in patches. A pack-mule caravan had arrived only ten minutes before and was now camping on this site. It consisted, as I learned later in the evening from one of the mule-drivers, of sixteen pack mules, three riding mules, and one horse. The caravan brought merchandise from the depot to villages in the jungle and in the sierra beyond the jungle. The muleteers were Indians, of course. There were three of them, who at the time we arrived were unloading the mules, while a boy of twelve was building a fire.

The pump-master's place looked a bit more colorful and lively than it had an hour ago. The pump-master was cleaning another lantern and when he thought it fine enough he hung it to a second post of the portico.

The music had not arrived. Every hope that it might still come had vanished by now. In the meantime, though, many men, women, and girls had appeared.

All the women were gaily dressed in bright-colored muslin gowns of the cheapest kind. They all wore stockings and high-heeled shoes, although on their way through the jungle they had taken off these fancy garments. None wore a hat. Yet most of them carried shawls, rebozos, or thin black veils to wrap round their heads on their way home in the cool and misty morning.

The men were clothed as always. Many were barefooted, a few had shoes, a few wore shabby puttees, while most of them had the ordinary home-made huaraches or Indian sandals on their feet. All their children had come with them.

Since these people had come for a dance, or at least to spend a jolly time, something had to be done.

Garcia had found an audience at last. Sitting on one of the few improvised benches outside the portico, close to a post from which a lantern was hanging, he fiddled continuously, going from one tune to another without any noticeable inter-mission. Nobody danced to the music he produced. He did not mind. He seemed fully satisfied, even happy, that there were people around who could hear him play and who had to listen

30

whether they liked it or not. No one yelled at him to stop the almost unbearable scratching and squeaking of his fiddle.

Everybody was waiting, but no one could say what he was waiting for. It looked as though all were expecting a great musician to arrive, who would provide a motive for an assembly of so many people, for the presence of these visitors now seemed without reason or sense.

Why, all the women had gone through really arduous pains for the occasion. They had washed themselves with perfumed soap; for hours and hours they had combed and brushed their hair; every rag they wore was clean; they had dressed themselves in the finest garb they owned, although their gauze dresses were the cheapest the Syrian peddlers carried—in spite of the fact that they cost so much that for many months the Indians would have to economize on everything. Then they had adorned their dresses and their hair with the most beautiful, the rarest flowers they could find. And then, to top it all, there had been the long, hard trip on mule or burro for five, six, eight miles through the steaming jungle, crossing swamps and wading rivers. And now all this seemed to have been in vain! It simply could not be. Everybody wanted to go home in the morning with many things to talk about for two months, it is so very lonely in those little settlements and hamlets hidden deep in the bush and jungle.

No one blamed the pump-master. He could not help it. He had done everything in his power to get the music. Besides, it would do nobody any good to blame anybody or anything for the failure of the party. It had to be: destiny's orders.

7

 The married women sat around on benches, on planks, on old sleepers, on gas drums, chatting and laughing.

The girls were giggling, watching the boys pass by, criticizing them, making fun of them, telling stories and exchanging bits of scandalous gossip about them. Now and then two or three girls would get up to stroll after some favored pair of boys, or they would pretend to pay no attention to them and walk in a different direction, knowing quite well that the chosen boys would follow them. After a while the girls would return and take their seats again. And when they sat down, other girls would arise to play the same game, the oldest in the world and the one that is still best liked, with or without motor cars and campuses, radios and night clubs.

The children were fighting, running around, rolling on the ground, chasing one another, crying, howling, watching the muleteers in their camp. A boy who had thrown stones at the others and hurt them was called by his mother; and he received a thrashing in public. While he got his ointment he

32

howled so much that the people around thought he was going to be butchered. No sooner was he set free than he hurried away to knock down the boys who had complained about him. This time, however, he kept out of reach of his dear mother's voice.

The bigger boys, those between twelve and fifteen, sat in groups, boasting of their strength and their abilities in general, and also about the size of the snakes, tigers, and lions they claimed to have met in the jungle when looking for stray goats or burros. Then they showed each other remarkable tricks—what they could do with their fingers, hands, arms, and bodies, how they could twist and contort them. Some were admired because they could turn their eyes in their sockets so that only the whites could be seen. Others told gruesome stories to the younger ones of how they had been swimming in the river and while diving had been caught by the leg by a bull alligator, and then they showed by throwing themselves on the ground and rolling about how they had freed themselves and what sort of fight they had had to go through before they found safety on the bank.

Everybody was smoking, men, women, children. But not the girls, because the boys say that a kiss from the tobacco-stained lips of a sweet girl is the ugliest thing in love. They smoked cigarettes made by rolling black tobacco in corn leaves. Mothers with their babies at their breasts blew tobacco smoke into the babies' faces to protect them against the mosquitoes.

The men lounged around in smaller groups, talking, laughing, boasting, and occasionally buying a bottle of beer for themselves and a lemonade for their womenfolk. They always had one eye on their women and daughters.

With Sleigh, the pump-master, and an Indian who worked with the oilmen, I stood mid-way between the bridge and the pump, slightly nearer to the river than to the pump-master's hut. I looked towards the river, but I could see neither it nor the bridge because of the blackness of the night.

From where I stood, by turning my eyes to the left I could see the fire of the mule-drivers' camp, where the boy at this moment was throwing coffee into the tin kettle by the fire while the men were toasting tortillas and cutting cheese and onions.

Dim lights shimmered through the brush on the opposite bank. As the soft breeze moved the shrubs, these little flickers now appeared, now disappeared in quick succession. These were mostly lights from the huts yonder where the women were making up for the dance, but some came from the big, tropical fireflies which were everywhere about us.

The boys sitting on the bridge at this end were still singing. Their stock of songs seemed inexhaustible, but the tunes seemed to be always the same. There were differences, though, and the Indians recognized them.

Wherever I looked there was animation and laughter and the noise of children at play.

8

  "I tell you, they are going to cement again, and they'll do it next week," Ignacio said importantly. He was the man who worked in the oil camp and was now standing with Sleigh and the pump-master and myself.

"How deep are you down now?" Sleigh asked.

"About twelve hundred feet, I think."

"At that depth there is no reason why they should cement the hole." The pump-master, who in fact knew nothing about oil, wished to impress us with his wisdom. He had picked up a few phrases which he had heard from oilmen passing by, so he went on bravely: "Why should they cement at twelve hundred? There are holes where they drill down to four thousand feet."

"You're telling me," Ignacio said, with the firmness of an old expert. He had been working with the oilmen only about three months and his principal job had been carrying iron pipes on his shoulders. "But, believe it or not, they are going to cement Monday or Tuesday. On that I'll bet any of you guys."

Garcia was still scratching his fiddle, but nobody paid any attention to his plaintive invitation to dance.

The singing of the boys on the bridge was getting thin, as if some voices had fallen out or as if all of them had at last become tired.

And at that moment something strange happened. I had the feeling that the air was invaded by a mysterious power which hovered over us like a huge winged beast. A kind of lethargy overcame the crowd. People began to yawn. And, as if by command, everyone suddenly stopped talking and laughing. There was a sense of tiredness and depression about us.

"You'll never make me understand why they should cement at twelve hundred feet." The pump-master brought up the question once more. To me it seemed that now he was not at all interested in what the oilmen were doing here or anywhere else in the world and that he was talking only to break that strange silence which was spreading around us.

None in our group accepted the pump-master's invitation to talk. The air was heavy, burdened as it is just before the break of a thunderstorm.

And then, when everybody was on the verge of opening his mouth to say something to end that horrible silence, there came the sound of a heavy splash from the river, which during the last fifteen minutes had been so quiet that not even the softest gurgle could be heard.

That plunge was very short, but distinctively characteristic in its peculiar sound. Yet nobody seemed to have noticed it. Nobody paid any attention to it. It was the sort of splash that occurred perhaps a dozen times every day.

I, however, felt as though the river had cried out: "Don't forget me, folks. I am still here and I shall survive all of you!"

I looked Sleigh straight in the face. He looked at me in the same manner. I knew he was thinking something and I wondered whether he might not be thinking the same thing I was. He had heard the plunge, but he tried to give the impression that he was paying as little attention to it as the others.

36

Now let me think. What was that sound? Could it be that one of the boys sitting on the bridge had jumped into the river just for fun? No, it was not that. I would have heard somebody swimming or paddling through the water. Yet there was no such sound after the big splash, nor was there any of the laughing or howling with which the other boys would inevitably have greeted such a plunge.

Perhaps it was a stone or a log thrown into the river by someone.

Garcia was fiddling again. His fingers must have been tired by now, but he fiddled on.

Perhaps it was a big fish jumping out of the water to catch a mouthful of mosquitoes. No, it was no fish. The sound was entirely different. If I could only find a simile for it! But I simply could not place it.

"Why are they going to cement?" Ignacio now said. "I'll tell you. They have already cemented two holes deeper in the jungle. You see, here's the way they work, those gringos. What they are actually doing is robbing our poor country, leaving us poorer still and making themselves a thousand times richer than they are already. They drill until they reach oil. No sooner do they get in than they right away cement the hole tight to keep the oil inside. Once they have it under control and locked up, then they come out and say that they have not found one drop, not even a noseful of gas. That's what they are doing, these damned foreigners of Americanos."

The pump-master shook his head. "No, that's something the gringos won't do. I know them too well. If they get to the oil, then they take it out, to the last crippled drop; they even dig out the mud and filter it for the oil left in it. What do you think, Don Nacho, how much does it cost them to drill a hole two thousand feet or perhaps deeper? That will cost them at least around thirty thousand dollars, and good American money too. Some holes cost them still more, up to fifty

37

thousand dollars Americanos. Do you think they would throw their good money away? If their money were pesos, maybe they would. But believe me, their money is good money, all dollars. So that's all squash about them drilling a hole and cementing it tight after they find oil."

Perhaps it was a dog. No, the dog is out. A dog would make lots of noise in the water. The boys would holler after him from all sides to make it tough for the animal, confuse him as to the shortest way to the bank. Yet there was not even the slightest noise after the plunge. Even a cat would have struggled and made some noise. But there was just the one brief, sharp splash, and nothing followed.

Ignacio laughed. He knew all the secrets of the American oil companies. "Only you, Don Agustín, because you are a maestro maquinista and have never had any experience with oil people, only you can talk the way you do. Can't you see, hombre, why they cement the hole at twelve hundred feet instead of going down to three or four thousand? Easy to see for one who is in the know, as I am. It is because they have struck oil already at twelve hundred, so they don't have to go down farther. That's why they cement now."

Manuel, the big brother from Texas, was standing by a girl, talking to her almost incessantly while she just giggled. He was different from all other boys she knew. She could see that. That was because he worked in Texas. He sees the wide world, and so he knows a pretty girl if he meets one. Out there in Texas he has learned how to tell the pretty and clever girls from the dumb ones. She let him understand clearly enough that she was willing any time he said so. Next time he came for a visit he would surely bring her a fine dress such as the gringo women in Texas wear all day long. He had become a genuine pocho up there in Texas, he even spoke American, and so she was immensely proud that he had chosen her for the dance tonight.

"Well, Don Nacho," the pump-master said, "you shouldn't

really tell me such things about gringos. As for me, all gringos may go to hell straight away. I don't give a peanut for any of them. Only you mustn't tell me that they are stupid. Whatever they are, even godless heathen who don't believe in the Holy Virgin, stupid they are not."

"I never said that they are stupid, Don Agustín. You mustn't turn my words round. I mean it just the opposite way, see? They are too smart, that's what they are. And that's exactly what I meant to say. If they would get no oil at twelve hundred, why should they cement? They would go down at least another twelve hundred to make sure. Otherwise they'd lose all that good money the hole has cost them so far. And now I'll tell you why they cement. It's a secret, but it's true just the same. You see, they have found oil and lots of it at twelve hundred. Now they cement it tight, but stake it as their legal property. They then say that they have struck nothing, not even a sneeze of gas. Why do they deny it? Because they haven't yet got leases on all the land around. If they now can make landholders believe that there is no oil on their properties they will get all the leases they want and they'll get them for a few hundred dollars. Otherwise companies with more money would come down and whip the prices for leases so high up to heaven that this company would have to let it go or spend a hundred times more than they spend now. As soon as they have got possession of all the leases they are after, then they return and break open all the cemented holes, and then you'll see the oil flowing like rivers in the rainy season."

The pump-master was convinced that he had underestimated the wisdom of his friend and neighbor Ignacio. His eyes widened, he looked admiringly at him and said: "Well, Don Nacho, I have to hand it to you. You are right after all. What you have told me right now, that must be correct, because it's exactly what I always expected that these gringos would do to us. Stealing not alone all our oil, but also all our land, that's what they do. For if they buy the leases for a hundred dollars instead of paying ten thousand, which is the real price, that's what I call a goddamned robbery. The government should know about that and of such dirty doings. Yet, as I've said before a hundred times over, stupid they're not. I see this clearer every day. They are not stupid, though I frankly admit that they are a damn bunch of bandits, and cabrones too."

"There you see, Don Agustín," Ignacio shouted triumphantly, "there you see, what did I tell you? You have only to open your eyes and ears when you're near them and you'll learn quickly and easily how they make big money. Yet they can't bedazzle me. Not me. None of them. I know those thieves all over."

That these people who were so very courteous by nature should, in the presence of Sleigh and myself, talk in such a way about Americans was proof that they did not count us among the gringos and thieves, simply because we were not oilmen, and therefore, in their opinion, we had no relationship with the race from which the oilmen come.

A man had meanwhile seated himself near Garcia. He had taken the fiddle away from him and put it against his breast, Indian fashion. All the girls looked up with hope in their eyes, because that man grasped the fiddle so resolutely, as though he were going to show Garcia how a fiddle should be played.

He played the first twenty notes so astonishingly well that the girls pulled at their dresses and stroked their hair, while the boys turned their faces quickly towards the benches and sleepers where the girls were sitting. Just when the boys were about to jump to their feet to dart over towards their partners, the tune got confused, and as abruptly as the music had begun, it finished with a pitiful moan. The new fiddler, trying to make good, started once more on another tune, but there was now no doubt that he was ten times worse than Garcia, who could at least keep time.

Garcia took his fiddle back with a smile. Tuning it, bending down to put his ear to the strings, he looked around at the crowd as if he wanted to say: "Well, now you can see for yourself who the really good musician is hereabouts."

He began playing again, and obviously influenced by the lively notes he had just heard, he fiddled with more energy. Two girls got up and started to dance. Garcia was in heaven when he saw that somebody was going to take his music seriously. After twenty passes or so the girls realized that it was impossible to dance to the mixed-up melodies Garcia was composing. If there were only a guitar at hand to accompany the fiddle, bad as it was, it might have been possible to obtain some sort of dance music.

Nobody thought of leaving the party. And what is more, no one showed any sign of disappointment. In fact, not a single person considered the party a failure. Real music to dance to would have been a good thing to liven up the party, but since it could not be had, everybody made the best of the gathering.

Most of the people there had come a long way. They couldn't return in so dark a night through the jungle; and since they were here anyway, everybody was sure that something would happen, because something had to happen to justify the trouble they had taken to get to the place. Where so many people are gathered together, something is bound to happen, and nobody and nothing can prevent it. It is nature's law.

We two, Sleigh and I, did not break into the discussion that was being held in our group, save occasionally to exclaim: "Zat so?" or "Really?" or "Maybe," or "No doubt!"

Ignacio, the man with the great knowledge of the way in which oil magnates make their millions, left us. He went looking for another group before whom he could show off. That he could win the admiration of the highly respected maestro maquinista would live in his memory for years to come, and the pump-master might now ask him for whatever he wished and he would get it. Men are devoted to those who admire them.

41

9

A young and very pretty woman came towards us. She was dressed in a cheap sea-green gauze frock. Through it one could see her white cotton petticoat, richly trimmed with lace. Two big red flowers adorned her thick black hair, combed and done up neatly, almost meticulously. A little bunch of wild flowers was pinned to her breast, and another was fastened at her girdle. One could see that she had good taste, for the flowers matched the color of her dress so well that a delicate but natural harmony was achieved. Her lips were painted a shade less than dark red. While many of the other women powdered their faces startlingly white, this woman had used ochre-colored powder. But like all the others she carried with her the heavy odor of the strongly perfumed soap bought from Syrian peddlers.

"Have you seen Carlosito?" She asked the question lightly, unconcernedly, as though she were not in the least interested in our answer and was asking it only to say something friendly. "He hasn't had his supper yet. He is too much excited because of Manuel's being here for the week-end. The kid forgets eating and everything." She laughed loud when she recalled the boy's fervor and she tried to imitate the way he acted. She waved both her arms through the air, and her feet were tripping and dancing on the ground. "Buenas noches, mamasita!" and "Adiosito, mamasita!" and "Cómo estas, mamasita linda, cielito?" and "I've got to run after my hermanitito Manuelito!" . . . "So he comes, so he goes, so he runs hither and thither, not for one minute remaining quietly in the same place. Off like the wind. I can't catch him and I can't grasp him. Well, that's the way kids are. Only he ought to have his supper, but he won't die if he skips it, will he?" She laughed not only with her face but with her whole body. "A happy mother if there is any," I said to myself.

The pump-master yawned, openly bored by the woman's fuss about her brat. He said: "He wasn't around here. I've not seen him since late in the afternoon when he came over to the wife to buy one centavito's worth of green chile."

"Yes, that's right. I sent him over here to get chile. That was long ago. He has been in the house since then twenty times or more. I'll catch him, never mind."

Sleigh looked around as uninterestedly as the pump-master did when he said: "I reckon he was here chasing other boys. Perhaps he wasn't. Well, the fact is I haven't noticed him, what with so many brats about."

"Never mind, caballeros, never mind at all. It isn't very important anyhow. When he's hungry he'll come home all right. He knows where he finds his beans ready waiting for him. It was only to say something. Forget it, caballeros."

The woman leaves us with a happy smile on her face.

A man walked slowly up to us, greeted us, and started to talk about the new boiler that had been promised the pump-master two years ago and which had not come yet and would probably not come for another two years.

Gazing after that pretty woman, I noticed that she was

43

going to Manuel, whom she spotted standing with his girl a short distance away from us. He listened to her and I saw him shake his head. Paying no further attention to the casual interruption, he talked again to his girl, whose happiness over having him for her companion did not diminish.

Without asking Sleigh, I now knew that this young pretty woman was the Garcia woman, the mother of the little Carlos and the stepmother of Manuel, who was only three or four years younger than she.

She walked over to the portico where her man was still sitting on the bench. He was not playing his fiddle at this moment, but was rolling himself a cigarette. He listened to her unimportant question with the mien of a man who has to listen to the same question a hundred times every day. While wetting his cigarette he shook his head, as if to say: "Don't bother me about that kid now, I've got other things to worry about at present."

For a minute the woman stood outside the portico, under one of the lanterns. She was obviously undecided what to do or where to go next. From the stillness of her body I judged that she was brooding over something, no doubt recollecting where and when she had seen the kid last, what he was saying or doing or telling her as to where he meant to go.

Now she slowly moved on, mixed with the crowd, looked this way and that, fixed her eyes on the boys of the age of Carlosito.

The farther away from the weak light of the two lanterns the men and women were, the more ghostly they appeared. Their deep bronze-brown faces blended with the surrounding darkness so perfectly that their faces vanished and only their hats and white clothes remained. One often got the impression that only clothes were walking about, over which hats were mysteriously hanging in mid-air.

Here and there I saw the Garcia woman walking among the groups. It seemed to me that she was now moving about

44

slightly nervously and that she jerked her head this way and that, pushing her face forward.

Garcia had taken up his fiddle again. Others had also tried to play during the last half-hour, but it was clear that Garcia was the best fiddler in the place.

Out from somewhere in the deep night the wailing tunes of a mouth-organ could be heard. Again girls aroused enough courage to try to dance, and again they realized, to their chagrin, that it was useless.

The pump-master woman, who had been sitting on a crude chair near the portico chatting with two other women, stood up, took down one of the lanterns, and went inside her hut.

With half the illumination gone, the square became darker and ghostlier than ever.

The campfire of the mule-drivers was nearly extinguished, and the three men and their boy came to the square to mix with the party. Right away they met several acquaintances and soon they were partaking in the general conversation.

The Garcia woman, coming from the direction of the bridge, stepped up to us at this moment. She walked fast now, as though she were in a real hurry. She said to us: "The kid isn't here and he isn't there. He isn't anywhere. I can't find him. Where do you think he might have gone?"

Her face, which only a quarter of an hour ago was so full of smiles and happiness, and ten minutes ago looked rather businesslike, had by now taken on an expression of worry and uneasiness. Yet it was not fear. She raised her eyebrows, opened her eyes wide, and with those staring eyes she gazed at us, searching the face of every one of us. And for the first time since I saw her, there appeared in her eyes a suspicion that we might know something or imagine something, and that we might be withholding our knowledge from her for some reason or other, perhaps out of sheer pity for her.

Helplessly, like a wounded animal that is down and can't get on its feet, she looked at us again, almost piercing our faces

45

with her burning eyes. Finding nothing, she shook her head and folded her hands against her breast.

Another change came over her eyes. The slight foreboding she had felt only a few seconds earlier had now become half a certainty. With all her power she tried to fight off that feeling, but she couldn't.

Well! The Great Music-Master had arrived. Here at last! He was ready to play. The dancing that all had been waiting for would begin. It would be a wild and whirling dance, to be sure. It would be a dance at which the trumpets and fanfares of Judgment Day would blare.

Slowly the dancers began to take their positions.

"Don't you worry, Carmelita," the pump-master said in a fatherly way. "That kid got tired out, so he has laid himself down somewhere as kids will do. There's nothing strange about that."

"He isn't at home. I've looked everywhere. I've searched every nook and corner."

"He'll be in another choza with other kids; sure, that's where he is."

"No. I've asked everywhere in all the jacales."

"Don't get hot, Carmelita. Perhaps he has crawled beneath a blanket or a petate or hidden in a heap of old sacks. He may have climbed up on the roof, where it is cool, and fallen asleep there."

The Garcia admits she has not thought of the roof. Frequently he climbs the roof of their hut or that of another, alone or in company with other boys. Why, only last night he slept on the roof. It is not comfortable to sleep on an inclined roof, but then, boys have their own ideas about comfort.

Hope entered the woman's mind. She hurried back across the bridge to the other bank.

The pump-master woman returned with the lantern. She hung it up again and once more the square was bright and the shadows retreated to the jungle.

46

10

 Garcia fiddled. He was not troubled by what was happening around him. A hundred times before, the kid had failed to come for his supper. And a hundred times he had had to search for him in the most unthinkable places where little boys may hide themselves. A dozen times if not more the boy had taken a burro and ridden away just for the fun of it. And he had done so knowing perfectly well that on returning he would be greeted with a good spanking.

Those womenfolk, hell, they always have their buttocks full of fear for no reason as soon as they haven't got their brats hanging at their skirts! Damn it! Although nobody tried any more to dance to his fiddling, he did not feel offended. Not at all. If someone thinks he can play any better why doesn't he show up? That's just it. There is nobody here who can play better. He would willingly and with pleasure lend him his fiddle, Garcia would. But there is no one. He alone can play. He knows all the foxtrots, all the one-steps, all the danzones, all the bostons and blues. They are, sorry to say, all mixed up a bit, one with another. You have to listen carefully for a while before you can make out what he is playing or what he means to play. If after hearing a dozen notes you are convinced he is playing a waltz, you realize that in fact he is playing a two-step. Never mind that, it is music all the same.

Now and then somebody played a mouth-organ again. You couldn't see the player. But you didn't have to see who it was that was performing in the darkness to know that the mouth-organ was going from one mouth to another, because between tunes you could hear the voices of the players. Often one heard what they were saying: "Caray, you burro, let me have it, you know nothing of music, a dumb ox plays better than you, you don't even know how to hold it the right way."

The boys on the bridge were singing no longer. From where I was standing I couldn't see whether they were still sitting on the bridge. Perhaps they were telling stories to one another. It might be that they had been attracted by the mouth-organ players and that they had joined them to try their skill as musicians.

Since we—Sleigh, the pump-master, another man, and my-self—were standing between the bridge and the pump-master's, it was only natural that anybody coming from the bridge should pass us on the way to the hut. When the Garcia returned from her search and walked up to talk to the pump-master woman, she saw us and stopped.

Her face had taken on the shimmer of fear. It was no longer mere anxiety, as it had been ten minutes before. Her wide-open eyes were fixed upon us questioningly. There was a tiny last flicker of hope still somewhere in the corners of her staring eyes. She did not want to ask the question lest that last shred of hope flutter away. She expected to hear from us that while she had been back at her hut we had learned something new about the whereabouts of the kid. None of us could resist her ques-tioning gaze any longer. It almost pierced my very soul.

I avoided her eyes and looked at her head. Her beautiful hair, combed and neatly done up when I had seen her first, was now deranged. She had climbed the roof and she had obviously crawled through shrubs near the hut.

"He isn't on the roof either, señores." We felt relieved of her eyes and we now breathed again as she spoke: "The neighbors also have searched for him in their homes. They haven't found him." This she said with the peeping voice of a little girl about to weep. "No, he isn't over there on the other bank." These last words were spoken as if each were weighted down by a heavy load.

For a few seconds she seemed not to know whether to expect an answer from us or not. She took a deep breath and walked over to her husband. Her steps had become less youthful.

While he fiddled unceasingly she talked to him with excited gestures. Suddenly she stopped and looked at him, anxiously awaiting his opinion.

He drew a last long stroke. Then, still holding the fiddle pressed against his breast above his heart (which is where every Indian musician holds his violin), he turned his head, and with his great, sad, dreamy eyes stared at his woman.

Suddenly his whole body grew tense. An Indian, considerably older in life and experience than she, he saw in her eyes far more than she wanted to let him see. She did not want to appear ridiculous before her man. It would be against the nature of an Indian woman. But he knew now what she could not and would not say. He opened his mouth and his lower jaw dropped as a dying man's does. Slowly, apparently without knowing what he was doing, he took the fiddle from his breast and let it rest on his left knee. And while he was putting down his fiddle he saw the Great Music-Master come and take it out of his hand. Garcia knew there would be music now, more music than he could stand.

The kid had been missing less than one hour. Many times he had been away from home for half a day, and for hours and hours nobody would know where he was roaming during that time. Yet never before had Garcia seen his woman with so much fear in her eyes.

"Manuel!" the woman called out.

Manuel came right away, shouting a few jolly remarks back to his laughing girl.

With laughter still in his voice he asked: "What is it, mother dear?"

"We can't find Carlos," she said with trembling lips. She looked sternly into his eyes, hoping to hear from him the only word that could relieve her of the growing pain in her heart.

The big smile on Manuel's face became a few degrees brighter when he said: "Why, mother, I saw him only a short while ago."

"Where?" the mother cried out, her face immediately lighting up as if a wreath of a hundred thousand sun-rays had fallen upon it.

"Where?" Manuel repeated. "Where? Why, right here. He wanted to blow his nose in my silk handker. He did it all right. Then he pushed it back into the hip pocket of my pants. Here, it's still there. Then he beat my legs with his fists, jumped with his new shoes on my toes to make me angry and make me box with him, and right then he was off again swift as a young coyote."

"You said only a short while ago, Manuelito."

"Of course, mother. Just now—only a few—I mean—just—wait. Or—"

"Or what? Or what? Speak up, Muchacho." The woman shook him violently by his arm. He was half a head taller than she.

"Or—wait—well, come to think of it, it might have been ten minutes, I should say, or fifteen."

The woman fixed her eyes on his lips to catch every word quicker than her ears would get them.

50

"Let me think, mother. I was talking all the time to Joaquina. And considering how much we talked in the meanwhile, well, it might be half an hour since I've seen the kid. Perhaps even longer. I believe, yes, I do believe it is longer still. Even an hour. Since then I haven't seen him. Not around here anywhere. That's right, mother, it may well be almost a full hour."

The face of the woman darkened. Then it seemed to shrink as if it were about to wither. Now her words tumbled out of her trembling lips: "After he had been here with you he came over once more. He gave me the thread I asked him for to tie up this little bunch of flowers on my dress. This happened after you had seen him."

In her growing fear she forced herself to think clearly and sum up every little detail she could remember and she tried to fit each into its proper minute, believing perhaps that by so doing she might find the exact minute when the kid had slipped away, as if knowing that exact minute might make it possible to find him. "Yes, yes, yes, this was afterwards. I know for sure it was later. Because he told me that he had pulled your handker out of your pocket and that he would have liked very much to steal it from you because it is such a beautiful silk handker and that he surely would have stolen it were it not that you are such a very good Manuelito whom he loves too much to steal anything from."

Manuel looked around the square, hoping to see his kid brother pop up that very second from the depth of the darkness to make faces at them. So vividly was the kid in Manuel's mind that he could not believe that anything serious had happened to him. Something so lively and so full of pep as that kid couldn't disappear like a feather. There must be a trace or a fight or a yell or something.

Garcia stood up slowly. For a while he did not know what to do. He had laid his fiddle on the bench. Feeling something in

51

his right hand he looked down and saw that it was the bow. He turned around and laid it close to the fiddle. Then he stared with empty eyes into the night.

The pump-master woman came up to Manuel and his stepmother. A few women followed her, and two men walked up to hear what had happened. So far only Garcia's family and we four men knew that the kid was missing.

The pump-master woman reasoned with the Garcia. She had children herself, she said, and there was not a day in the year when she didn't have to work to find one or the other, and more often than not in places where no Christian soul would ever think a child might be. Why, they had even been found inside of hollow trees, and no one on earth knew how they wriggled in, since the hole was too small and they had to be cut out with an ax. "Children, dear me, don't tell me anything about children, least of all about little boys. Once we found our Roberto inside the boiler and it was only by a holy chance that the boiler was inspected before water was poured in and the fire started."

Other women, all mothers, made fun of the Garcia woman's fear, telling her she wouldn't worry so much if she had a dozen brats and not just this one. "Don't tell me anything about these little rascals," one woman said; "these little vermin and good-for-nothings return home always. That's just the trouble with them. I wish some of mine would stay away for good and look out for themselves. Don't you get excited, Carmelita. As soon as he gets hungry he will be back and will make a big row if he doesn't find his frijoles and tortillas ready for him. A boy like that can't just fly off like a mosquito, seen by nobody. You'll see him soon enough and then give him a good whipping so that he knows where he belongs. They are like puppies, that's what they're like."

Manuel had walked away. After a few minutes we heard him calling in the darkness: "Carlos! Carlosita! I've got candy,

52

Carlosito! Where are you? I got candy, Carlos. Carlosito!" His voice went farther into the night and finally was heard no longer.

Talk ceased. Everybody listened for an answer from the kid. Yet there was only the whining, the singing, the chirping, the humming from the jungle, at intervals interrupted by Manuel's distant shouts.

Stirred up by Manuel, other groups on the square became interested in what was going on. They all began to move, to fall in line for the dance to which the ghostly music was playing faster every minute.

The pump-master went to the open shed where the pump and the boiler were located. With lighted matches he peered into every corner. Those who were near him watched his every move and expected him any minute to drag out the boy from some hidden retreat behind or under the pump. On seeing him return empty-handed, everybody thought it very silly to have believed the kid to be under the pump or inside the boiler or in the ash pit.

The Garcia looked pitifully from one to another. Holding one fist against her mouth, she nibbled thoughtlessly at her fingers. Her eyes were like an animal's which sees some danger approaching and finds itself without means of defense. A certain thought entered her mind. She took her fist away from her face and hid it in the palm of her left hand. For a while she pressed both hands against her breast. With a jerk she turned around and hurried towards the bridge. After a few paces she stopped. In utter despair she let her head drop. Slowly her arms glided down her body until they dangled lifelessly. She turned away from the bridge and with heavily dragging feet she came back to our group.

Old man Garcia was standing with us, and not knowing what better he could do, he began rolling a cigarette.

"Carlos! Carlosito! Carluchito!" Now from this direction,

then from that, sometimes nearer, sometimes far away, Manuel's strong voice could be heard calling his kid brother.

Only the jungle answered with its whining.

The boys, spurred by Manuel's anxious search, formed half a dozen groups of two and three and scattered in all directions. Soon from everywhere one heard "Carlosito!" After each call there was silence for a few seconds so that little Carlos might have his chance to answer, were it ever so faintly. It seemed that even the jungle fell silent for a moment as if it wanted to help save a little child.

11

 "Señora! Señora Garcia! Señora Garcia!" The bright and jubilant voices of two boys broke the monotony of the calling of the child's name. These young voices freshened up the heavy atmosphere like a cool breeze wiping the depressing glow off a treeless plain at the height of a midsummer day. And again those animated and exultant voices blared through the night like the cornets of a military band. Running like devils, the two boys, shouting and yelling all the time, were now crossing the bridge.

"Well, well! Now, there, there! There is the boy at last," the pump-master woman cried out, and blew a deep sigh of relief. "Haven't I said a hundred times that a healthy boy like him can't get lost? Well, thanks to heaven, that's all over now!"

All faces lost their funny distortions and became ordinary human faces again. Hurriedly uttered words were flying about all groups. Everybody wished to say something very quickly and wanted to confirm that he had said so long before. Some even went so far as to boast that they had known all the time where the boy had been hidden.

55

A few youngsters and girls left the center of the square, bored now with all that noise about nothing. It was pure nonsense, the whole excitement was, for how could it be possible that a boy would disappear with a hundred people around?

The Garcia swallowed something which had been in her throat for a long time. Then she licked her dried lips. After this she took a deep breath as if she had not breathed for an hour. Somehow, though, she was not fully taken in by the joy of relief shown by all the others. There was hope rising in her soul, but doubt remained the stronger emotion within her. So hard had she worked her mind into the certainty that her boy was lost that now she had some difficulty in giving her thoughts a new direction. She was perhaps not clear as to her true feelings at this moment. Yet deep in her heart there was something in which her doubts found nourishment. One could read it from her eyes, in which doubt and suspicion mingled with bits of hope and a slight expectation of the best.

The two boys arrived at our group. Breathlessly they said: "Señora Garcia, you are looking for your chiquito, for your little Carlos, aren't you, señora?"

"Yes, yes, of course, she is. We all have been looking for him a long time." It was not the Garcia who answered the boys; it was other women in our group who pressed the boys for a quick report. "Well, where is he? Come, come! Out with it."

The Garcia was staring at these two boys as if they had come from another world.

"Carlos has ridden to Tlalcozautitlan, that's where he has gone," the elder of the two boys said, stumbling over his own words, so hurriedly and breathlessly were they spoken.

"Yes, that's true," confirmed the younger one, "that's absolutely true, Señora Garcia, cross my heart and soul."

"Well then, everything is all right now," the pump-master

56

woman said, slapping the Garcia on her shoulders in a neighborly way.

"Didn't I say so long ago?" another woman broke in. "A boy can't fall out of the world just like that."

The men said nothing. Most of them left us to go back to other groups where they wanted to take up their interrupted discussions.

The Garcia frowned as if she had great difficulty thinking. Holding both her hands against her abdomen, she looked at the two boys without speaking.

The boys were getting slightly irritated under this piercing stare and they tried to run away. The Garcia, however, grasped one of the boys by his arm and so the other boy remained also.

"You say he rode to Tlalcozautitlan?"

"Yes, señora, he really and truly has."

"On what did he ride to Tlalcozautitlan?"

"On a horse, señora."

"On whose horse? On whose horse can he have ridden away?" The Garcia questioned the boys with a deadly calm, almost frightening voice. A woman condemned to death, with only one hour to live, might question in this calm, direct way a newly discovered, very important witness on whose testimony the governor's decision for a stay depended.

"Whose horse was it?" She repeated her question, since neither of the boys had answered yet.

Now the elder said: "A boy bigger than me was coming this way, and he was riding on a beautiful white horse."

"Yes, that's right, señora," the younger one said, "he was sitting on a beautiful white horse and Carlos was standing right here by my side and the big boy on the white horse said—"

"—and the boy on the white horse said," the elder boy took up the tale again, "he said: 'Won't you come with me, Carlos? I am riding very fast.'"

"And what did Carlos answer?"

" 'Are you riding to Tlalcozautitlan?' Carlos asked. To this the boy on the white horse said nothing and only nodded his head. Then Carlos said: 'That's fine, because then I might ride with you to Tlalcozautitlan and buy myself lots of candy; you see, I have twenty centavitos given me by my big brother who has come today for a visit from the far Texas land.' So then the boy on the white horse said: 'All right, let's go, my horse is a very fast one, awfully fast, we will be there in no time.' And saying so, he helped little Carlos up on his horse, and the very moment he had done so, the horse was away like nothing and we couldn't see it any more."

Whenever one of the boys telling the story stopped or hesitated, the other one took up the tale and went on with it. From all appearances the story seemed to be true. Two boys of their age are not able to tell a false story the way these two boys were narrating it.

The Garcia searched the boys' faces. The boys looked into her eyes with frankness. Then the Garcia looked at the faces of the people standing by, glancing from one to another although their faces could not be seen clearly.

Manuel arrived at our group. A few boys had gone after him and told him there was news at the pump-master's.

The Garcia woman looked at him. Then she turned violently round to the two boys and said, almost yelling: "I don't believe it!" Again she shouted: "I don't believe it. Carlos does not ride away from home, not when Manuel is here and when he knows that Manuel has to leave early Monday morning. He will not miss a minute to be with Manuel. And if he really wanted to go to Tlalcozautitlan he would have come first to Manuel and told him so and made him go with him."

"But it is true, señora, he rode away with that big boy," the elder boy insisted.

"Who was that boy?" the Garcia asked suddenly.

58

"We don't know."

"Is that so? You don't know him, you don't even know that boy?"

"No, we don't know him, señora," the elder boy repeated. And the younger answered: "I saw him once pass by here with a loaded burro, but he didn't stop here, not even for a drink of water did he stop, as all the travelers coming this way do."

The pump-master came close and asked: "What did the boy on the horse look like?"

Up to now the two boys had been very clear about everything they had been describing. But in trying to answer this new question they became more and more confused and even contradicted each other. Neither remembered exactly what that boy looked like. Asked if he was an Indian boy or a Mexican or a white, they said they had not looked closely enough and it was too dark to see whether he was Indian or white, and that they had looked more at the beautiful horse than at him. They could not, when questioned further, even describe the saddle cn which he was sitting. The younger boy insisted the horse had no saddle, while the elder said it was saddled. Nor could they say anything about how the boy was dressed. Then again, the time they gave as to when the boy invited Carlos for the ride, fitted into the time when the kid had last been seen. According to the two boys, it was now one hour since Carlos rode away. This would mean it had been eight o'clock. And it was exactly eight when the child left the hut and ran as fast as a weasel towards where he knew Manuel and his father were. Since that moment his mother had not seen him again.

All those present save the mother believed the story of the two boys, especially since a dozen men declared that they had seen several men riding by, some of them riding in the direction of Tlalcozautitlan. Everybody added that the two boys had no reason whatever to tell such a story and in so serious a

59

situation, that they gained nothing by telling it except maybe a good thrashing if they were found out to be lying deliberately.

Garcia wakened from his lethargy. He looked for a horse to take him to Tlalcozautitlan. It was quite possible that the boy on the horse was traveling farther than just to that little town and on reaching it he might have left Carlos there all by himself. Boys play such tricks on other boys, especially smaller ones. They never think of the consequences of such tricks. All the stores in that town were closed by now and there was never any light in the streets. Little Carlos was perhaps at this moment sitting in a dark corner, forlorn and either crying or asleep. If perchance he were picked up by good people he couldn't even tell where he lived. Because this settlement had no name and was not to be found on even the best map. It was just "Huts by the River," and of such places there are thousands in the republic.

Garcia's activity—saddling the horse, mounting it, listening to a score of opinions as to which was the shortest and best trail, for there was no road—filled the Garcia woman with new hope. At least she thought it was hope, while in fact it was only that for a few minutes her thoughts were moving in another direction. She felt easier knowing that her man was on the way to find the boy at the place where everybody assured her he was. She sat down with other women on a bench and soon she joined their talk about everyday things.

Manuel leaned against a tree-trunk. He, at least for the present, had no desire to mix with the girls, as all the other boys were doing now that the excitement was over. But after ten minutes he walked slowly back to his pretty girl, and both soon disappeared where the shadows were deepest.

Sleigh had shown little interest in the whole affair. I wondered what could get him aroused to some sort of enthusiasm. Sometimes I thought him just brain-lazy. Then again I thought him a wise man who had learned that nothing matters, not even his own death. He was interested in his cattle. That was true. But I often doubted even that interest, for he probably showed concern about the cattle only because he was hired to attend them. Yet maybe he really loved the cattle and did not wish anybody to know it. When the excitement was at its peak he said to me that he had better go to his house to see whether the missing cow had come in. He returned in time to hear the two boys telling their story. After this he helped Garcia fetch a horse and saddle it.

Now he was again standing with me, telling me in his slow drawl that the goddamned cow had not come home yet and that he would give anything to know where that cow might be at this time of night.

12

A boy called for Manuel. After a while Manuel came out of the dark and I went closer to hear what the boy wanted of him.

"It isn't true at all, Manuel, that Carlos rode to Tlalcozautitlan," the boy said. "I know that Carlos and another boy have ridden to Pacheco, and they did not ride a horse, but just a burro."

"Did you see that?" Manuel asked skeptically.

"Sure, I saw it or I wouldn't be telling about it. Do you think me a liar, or what?"

"Why didn't you tell it before?"

"Simply, I didn't know that those two boys had told you Carlos had ridden to Tlalcozautitlan."

The Garcia heard his last words. She jumped up and ran over to us.

Shaking the boy wildly by his shoulders, she cried: "What did you say right now?"

The boy repeated his tale and swore by all the saints that he had seen Carlos riding away with another boy on a burro and that they had taken the trail which leads to Pacheco.

The Garcia let her head sink between her shoulders. Her whole body shrank. Her mouth was wide open and her eyes flickered like a madman's.

The pump-master grasped her by the arm and shook her. He said: "Now, don't you get excited over nothing Carmelita, please, calm down. Don't let your worry eat you up. Wait until your man is back from Tlalcozautitlan. There is nothing, absolutely nothing you can do until he has returned."

The woman said nothing. It was obvious she had heard not a word.

One of the mule-drivers who were camping there said: "I know the way to Pacheco. It's an awful trail by day and ten times worse at night. If you don't know it very well, you have no chance to return at night. Now, I say, if somebody will lend me a mule—a horse won't do—I'll ride over to Pacheco and look for the kid. Our mules are tired, they can't make it, not that trail, tired as they are."

A mule was offered immediately. When he mounted, a boy riding a burro came up and said that he wished to accompany him because he, too, knew the trail.

"Have you guys enough matches?" the pump-master yelled after them. They would have to make torches to light them across difficult stretches on that hard trail.

"We've plenty," they shouted.

The Garcia looked into the darkness into which those two had just disappeared. She dug her fingers into her hair and turned round to face again the pump-master's hut. The little shred of hope she had had for a few minutes, when everybody was so confident that the kid must be in Tlalcozautitlan, was gone entirely. Her hope was never very strong anyway. That certainty she had had the first minute she missed the boy seized her again. What nobody else under heaven could know, she, his mother, knew right away, that the boy was never coming back. Her heart and her instinct, that instinct of a primitive, of an Indian mother, told her the truth.

Everybody else here might doubt, but she no longer doubted. In fact she had never doubted. She had only been playing so as to keep herself from going mad.

And now, being certain, she became herself once more. The flickering disappeared from her eyes. She pulled herself together as if by a resolute decision. There was work to do now. She had to do something for her baby. She had to get busy. Whatever might have happened, she had to see her darling once more, once more she had to hold him in her arms, press him against her heart, and cover his sweet little face with kisses. She had to get him, even if she should have to drag him out of the clutches of hell. But she had to get what was left of him.

With firm steps she hurried across the bridge back to her hut. One minute later she was crawling with a lantern in her hand among the shrubs along the opposite bank of the river. Now she disappeared deeper into the bush, now she returned to the bank. With the lantern dangling from her hand she stretched her arm over the river to light up the muddy water. She called her baby by the sweetest names she could think of or her heart was able to invent. Seen from this side, where I was standing, every move she made looked ghostly. Everybody expected soon to hear a cry which would be horrible and gruesome.

For half a minute she stood still by the bank, thinking of what had to be done. Her arms were hanging motionless. In her right hand she held the lantern. It lit up her dress. But her face was partly in shadow, and it resembled no face I ever saw before. It might have been a face created by an insane sculptor who had tried to outsmart nature.

On this side people were gathered close to the bank, looking at the lonesome mother who, with a lantern, wanted to get back her baby. Two enemy camps divided by the river, two worlds opposed to each other. One world was in deepest sorrow and pain, the other world ready to help yet none the less happy, in a way, that it was the other world which had been floored by a merciless fate.

A few men crossed the bridge to join the lonely mother. Aimlessly they crawled through the shrubs and brush. They didn't really believe they would find the kid there. They merely wished to show the mother that they were willing to do all in their power to lessen her sufferings.

The mother came back towards us. As she crossed the bridge she held the lantern over the river, but the light hardly penetrated the muddy yellow water.

The pump-master woman walked over to her, put one hand upon her shoulder, and said: "Let's wait, Carmelita dear, and see first before we worry so much. Come, sit down by me on the bench and don't worry and break your head to pieces. The kid has really ridden away with that boy, I'm sure of it. We may worry later a good deal if the men come back without having found a trace of him. Yet they'll find him all right. With all that worry now we can do nothing. Just wait and see."

"Carlos hasn't ridden away," the Garcia said, firmness and conviction in her voice. "He does not ride away when Manuel is home."

"Tut, tut, Carmelita! There, there! Children, dear me!" The pump-master woman laughed loudly. "You have got only that one. What do you know about these brats? I know better, I've five. What you never even dream of, that's exactly the first thing they'll do."

The Garcia put her lantern on the ground by her feet. She turned her head towards the river and with tired, heavy eyes looked into the darkness. Then she faced again the group of women she was standing with, and looked from one to another without saying a word. Though she was in the midst of neighbors and friends, she felt utterly alone in the world. Her

65

head drooped and she closed her eyes for a few seconds. Then suddenly her body stiffened and she cried out: "The boy is in the river! The boy has been drowned!"

Everyone present stood aghast, as if lightning had struck near by. Some women crossed themselves. The pump-master woman fought to catch her breath, and finally gasped: "Carmelita, for heaven's sake, by the Most Holy Virgin and Her Holy Child Jesu Cristo our Lord and Master, don't commit such a horrible sin against God. How can you say such a terrible thing? Have you gone mad, woman? Come to, come to, woman!"

The Garcia uttered a deep sigh. She felt relieved of the thick lump in her throat which had been trying to choke her for the last half-hour. She stretched her neck and moved her head round in a wide circle to free herself still more from that nightmare. Her eyes became sober, almost brutally sober. She was at last herself.

While everybody was still dumbfounded, the Garcia started explaining, so clearly and fluently that one might think she had memorized it. She was getting rid of all her anxiety by talking fast, by summing up all her thoughts concerning the whereabouts of her baby.

"How excited that kid was this evening and the whole afternoon! Never have I seen him like that. Wild, swift, uncatchable. I might have chained him to a post and he would have broken away, so wild he was. He had practically lost all sense of what he was doing and where he was running. I couldn't keep him in the house for more than two minutes at a time. He had to run across to Manuel again. And off he went like a whirlwind. He knows the way to the bridge, and the bridge itself, well enough—better perhaps than any one of us—because ever since he could run at all he has been running across that bridge two hundred times every day. So he ran back again without even thinking that he might ever fall off the bridge, because he could run across it blindfold. But now he had the new shoes on his little feet, those pretty shoes with polished and lacquered soles that he was so proud of. With these shoes on his feet he was not the same any more. But how could he know that? No longer was he sure about his way, and no longer did he have his feet under control the way he used to when he ran barefooted. How could he, a child, know the difference it makes to your feet when you have shoes on? Now, when I crossed the bridge tonight, I almost tumbled over. I saw the lantern hanging here at the pump-master's and went straight towards the light. Only when I stumbled against the rim and almost lost my balance did I remember that the bridge doesn't lead straight towards the choza here, but more to the right. When this happened to me, right then my first thought was that should the kid run so wildly and thoughtlessly across the bridge, as he surely did because of his excitement, there is every chance that he might tumble over the rim and fall into the river. That's why, on coming over here, my first question was about the kid. Otherwise, if this had not happened to me, I would not have thought of him, not until I saw him here again. And believe me, all of you, when I asked for the boy and nobody had seen him, I knew instantly that it was too late already, for my heart was full of a sudden pain."

Nobody interrupted the mother in her long speech. For many minutes no one said anything. They were thinking of what they had just heard. There was so much good sense in what she had said that most of those present were beginning to believe that what had happened was just as the mother had explained it.

The pump-master woman was the first to speak. "Now listen, Carmelita, be reasonable. What you tell us is absolutely impossible. It can't be. Somebody would have heard it when the kid tumbled over and fell into the river. There would have been a splash, sure there would."

Tumbling over. Falling into the river. A plunge. A splash. I looked sideways and my eyes met those of Sleigh, who was looking at me at that very moment. Neither of us had any desire to say anything.

"No, no, that's quite impossible," a man said, "we would have heard it. If such a boy falls into the water he splashes, doesn't he? Has anyone heard such a splash? I, for one, haven't. Besides, a boy of his age doesn't tumble into the water and disappear immediately just like that. He would shout and yell like hell. He would beat and kick around and make such a terrific noise that you could hear it a mile away. No, don't tell me he is in the river, not me."

"Naturally, he would make an awful noise," the pumpmaster remarked. "I know that kid, I do. There wasn't a day in the year when he wasn't in the water swimming and splashing and making such a row that you would think he owned the whole river all by himself. In the water he is like a fish, the kid is. He would have got out just like that, shoes on or no shoes on. And if he had met with some difficulty he would have hollered like the very devil himself, that's what he'd have done."

The Garcia had listened to every word; not once had she interrupted the talk. Now, however, she felt that she had to defend her boy. "Certainly he would have worked himself out of the river, and all alone, and he would have yelled, too, if he couldn't get out. But how could he yell? He was wearing his new shoes, so he wasn't safe on his feet. Running across the bridge fast as he could and not thinking of anything but of Manuel. And so he stumbled with his shoes against the rim. Had he been barefooted, he would have got hold somehow. But the soles were smooth and polished like a mirror. Before he even realized what was happening to him he had already tumbled over and had knocked his head against the rim or against a post. So he became unconscious instantly, and before he could come to, he was already under the water with his belly full and his windpipe choked. He never got any chance to make a noise."

Having told her story so as to make everyone see that she was not out of her mind, the Garcia had nothing more to say. Nobody could convince her that the kid might be somewhere else. She knew he was in the river and she had to get him out. That was all she was thinking of now.

13

The men or women were by no means satisfied
with the Garcia's narrative. They said she was just
seeing things because she was not herself any more. Someone
remembered the boys who had been sitting on the bridge and
singing at about the time when Carlos was supposed to have
fallen into the river. These boys declared that they had seen
nothing and heard nothing, and that they were sitting at the
end of the bridge on this side, facing the water and thinking
only of their songs; but they were positive that the kid could
not have fallen in the river without their seeing or hearing it.
Of course, they added, the night was so black that they could
not have seen the kid if he had been half the length of the
bridge away from them. They would have paid little attention
to a splash because they were fully occupied with their singing.
After all, fish jumping out of the water to catch flies and
mosquitoes make the same noise.

"Now, there you can hear it for yourself, Carmelita," the
pump-master said; "these youngsters have been sitting here near
the spot during the whole evening and they haven't heard a

70

thing, not the slightest splash. So you see you are just making up a story which has no foundation. It simply couldn't have happened the way you imagine."

The Garcia was silent.

Everyone produced another idea with which to convince the Garcia that she was wrong. No one supported her.

A couple of men, noticing that I had not joined the discussion, asked me bluntly what I thought of the Garcia's tale. I knew where the kid was. Sleigh knew it too. I saw him shrug his shoulders as if he wanted to answer on my behalf. Then I spoke. "What can I say, amigos? I don't know all the nooks and corners, holes and trees and tunnels around here where a little boy might hide himself. So what can I say? Anybody might fall in the river; why not a boy?"

"Well, then, do you really think he may have fallen in the river?"

"I've told you my opinion. It's possible. Anything under heaven is possible. Therefore it is also possible that the kid may have fallen in the water. Where there is water, anybody may fall in any time, whether he wants to or not. That's the way with all water."

"The señor is perfectly right," a man next to me said. "Don't you folks remember—it's only a year back—when in this river, only two miles farther down, the Egyptian was drowned?—I mean that Egyptian who had his choza there and who planted onions and lettuce for the market."

"Yes, I remember it well," another stated, "but the circumstances were entirely different. That Egyptian was taking a bath in the river and he unexpectedly reached a deep washout or some sort of whirlpool into which he disappeared and never came up again."

An old Indian was nearing our group. He came close and asked me: "What do you think, señor, what we might do and what we should do?"

Half a hundred people were talking and denying and talking again, yet none had suggested anything practical. The old Indian was the first to do so.

"Since you ask me, I would advise that the river be searched along both sides of the bridge and also for a hundred fifty feet or so down the stream. If the kid really is in the water, then we'll find him and so we'll know at least where he is. What is more, if the men who have gone in search of him return and have not found him in either place and in the meantime we have not discovered him in the river, then we will know that we have to search the whole jungle."

The Garcia had crossed the bridge again. With the lantern in one hand she was standing at the other end of the bridge. After a while she went close to the rim and held the lantern as far out over the water as she could. Suddenly she let out a horrible scream.

A few boys ran across to her.

They came back right away, tapped their heads, and said: "The señora must have gone nuts, for nothing is in the water."

It was hardly necessary to tell us that, for even if the kid were in the water at that particular spot, the Garcia would not have been able to see him, so muddy was the water, so dim the light of the lantern.

Nevertheless, the Garcia now yelled continuously. No sooner had she finished one of those long plaintive cries than she uttered another, still more plaintive, still longer. It was the crying of a primitive Indian woman bewailing the death of a loved one. It wasn't weeping, it was a howl which seemed to accuse the heavens. It was the howl of an animal whose mate or child has been killed. But I recognized in that almost savage howl the same deep sorrow that one finds in the silent weeping of an American woman.

If all the women here had been convinced that the kid had been drowned, they would have joined the Garcia in her

72

lamentation. And they would have joined her with all the compassion that mothers and wives are capable of when they open their hearts and souls to the suffering and pain of another mother or another wife. For only a mother and wife knows what a mother and wife suffers when bemoaning the loss of someone beloved. Because what befalls one mother, the same befalls every other mother on earth at the same moment, wherever she may live, for in all eternity it is never just one single woman, a Garcia woman in a Central American jungle, who is in deep pain, but it is always all womanhood that suffers and weeps.

No other woman here was sure of the kid's death. They remained quiet. Some called their little ones to them as if they might be in danger, and they held their babies against their breasts as the safest place on earth they could offer them.

Two men crossed the bridge and, ever so delicately and lovingly, led the Garcia woman back to this side and made her sit on a bench in the pump-master's portico.

The pump-master woman gave her water to drink, sat beside her, and, in a motherly way, stroked her hair and occasionally dried her tears with the ends of her shawl.

The men were standing around, once more wondering what to do and how to behave in this situation. They were uneasy in the presence of a mother who had lost her baby and who, in spite of all the sympathy shown her, was alone in the world. They had a feeling of guilt, they shuffled about and tried to hide themselves. No one spoke. Whenever the woman cried out again, the men's faces became distorted. Their uneasiness became finally so unbearable that they began to do what every man on earth does when he finds himself superfluous. They got very busy about nothing in particular.

Without uttering many words and without waiting for a leader, they ran like ants this way and that. Some carried timber, others took their machetes and went into the bush to get more wood. Huge fires were lighted on both banks and arranged so that both sides of the bridge were illuminated. One stripped and waded into the river. He started diving alongside the bridge. It was a daring job and might easily have cost the diver his life.

The river-bed was boggy and covered with all sorts of plants, partly tropical water shrubs, partly shrubs and bushes torn away from the banks far upstream and caught by the bridge posts when they were carried down by the current. This marine jungle was infested with water snakes, crabs, and young alligators, not to mention the hundreds of other tropical underwater creatures.

The swimmer who keeps to the surface will rarely be in danger, but a diver may easily be caught. Yet, a few minutes later, another man stripped and started diving too. Soon there were six bronze-brown human bodies in the water. Women and girls lined the river-banks and the bridge to watch the naked men searching for the kid. The lean, brawny bodies, which looked youthful in spite of the fact that most of the men were fathers, seemed to be covered by a metallic gold film. Their thick, long, wiry hair appeared still blacker and thicker when their heads popped up on the surface. Breathing deeply, they gazed up to the bridge, where men and women were watching them, and said not a word. But one could easily read in their dark brown eyes the answer to the unspoken question: "Nada! Nada! Nothing, nothing!"

Among the men in the river there now appeared a very old Indian with white hair. His body, while still well formed and lean, was less brawny, less agile and flexible than those of the others. His skin was less golden. And his chest was not so strong. Hence he could not stay under water as long as the young could. Yet whenever the others, the young ones, showed signs of getting tired, he was the one who fired them on again.

74

Carrying a long iron hook tied to a lasso, the pump-master strode up to the bridge. Slowly he walked along the rim, constantly throwing in the hook and dragging it along the bottom. Whenever he thought he had caught something, he pulled it up—to find only some weeds or twigs.

Sleigh was standing near the pump.

I went up to him and said: "If we only had a boat, more might be done. A pity that the pump-master hasn't got one."

"There is a boat down the river that belongs to a Dutchman who raises chickens and grows tomatoes there and never makes any money. He has a boat all right, home-made. But it is at least three miles from here, if not four. And what is worse, the trail can't be made before the sun comes up."

We walked together to another group where Sleigh started talking about things which had nothing to do with the kid. He was right. One cannot talk all the time about the same thing; you have to go on living, boy dead or no boy dead.

14

 It was a picture—a picture exuberant in its great-
ness, in its truthfulness, in its liveliness, in its colors,
in its constant changes.

On both banks huge bonfires were flaring. They threw their
flames high up into the air and flickered in the mild breeze. A
hundred different shadows, long and short, bulky and thin,
darted now this way, now that, now playing upon the ground,
then sweeping over the water or along the bridge, until at last
they were swallowed up by the jungle walls—only to shoot
out again two seconds later. On the bridge a score of men and
boys were lined up, holding torches and flaming sticks over
the water. Others were running like deer up and down the
banks to start new fires or to bring light to a diver who was
shouting for it. Long pennants of smoke followed these torch
runners.

Bronze-brown men and youngsters were hurling fresh fuel
into the fires. Swarms, thousands, millions of sparks rose
towards the dark sky.

Here and there boys were kneeling on the bridge, leaning

with their torches far over the rim, and a black head dripping with water would appear on the surface of the muddy river.

Women and girls gaily dressed in their cheap but bright-colored dance gowns, with crowns of beautiful wild flowers on their heads and with little bunches of flowers fastened on their breasts and girdles—many of the women carrying babies in their arms, others leading children by the hand—were wandering back and forth across the bridge. Now and then half a dozen people would suddenly run to a definite spot on the bridge, where someone was shouting as if he had seen or found something of importance.

Little clouds and flags of smoke were flying over our heads like strange night birds, like fairies, like ghosts trying to materialize and falling apart at the same moment.

The surface of the river seemed to be bedecked with thousands of floating gold coins. Into that river of gold, naked human bodies were diving. Here they came out again, swam to a bridge post, wiped the water off their faces, and shook their thick black hair. There one diver was hanging on to the post with one hand while with the other he pulled thorns off his legs. One diver left the water and went to a fire to warm his hands and feet, which had become numb. With his back to the river and his face to the flames, he stretched out his arms to the fire and closed and opened his hands quickly, while a friend of his put a lighted cigarette between his wet lips.

A child that had been asleep awoke and whined. Another child, awakened by the first, began to cry. Their mothers ran up to feed them from their breasts.

Most of the children had fallen asleep. They lay on the ground near the portico, huddled together in groups to keep warm and feel safe. Some of the children were wrapped in a blanket as if they were sticks. Others were covered with ragged pieces of cotton cloth. Some were lying on mats of the kind put between the saddle and the back of a horse. Others were sleeping on old sugar sacks. Many were stretched out on the bare sandy ground.

The bigger children were, of course, having the time of their lives. Here they were watching the divers. There they were betting on which of the divers would stay longest under water. Others were more interested in the bonfires and torches. A few practical jokers of the next generation were playing nasty little tricks on smaller boys and girls. Some boys who had never had a chance were now at last testing their skill as musicians on the mouth-organs snatched from the trousers left ashore by the divers.

So it appeared that everybody had his own kind of fun and was making the best of a party which two hours before had looked like a complete flop. Even the mules of the caravan were partaking of that lively affair in their own fashion.

They were grazing near the banks. Now and then they brayed sadly into the night and were answered by others out on the prairie. Frequently, when they got in the way of the men who were busy near the river, they got kicked in the hams. Yet they took it as a friendly gesture and did not move—until they themselves decided to change places, which is the way the stubborn always win.

The night was getting cool.

Aided by a neighbor, the pump-master woman was in her kitchen making coffee. A very fine kitchen it was. All the neighbors agreed to that. The kitchens of all the huts in the settlement on the opposite river-bank were far less luxurious. No one else had his kitchen separated from the main room, which in all the homes was the only room. The fact that the pump-master had a separate kitchen proved that he was of a higher class. The hearth was a wooden case filled with earth, like Sleigh's. The pump-master and Sleigh were the only people in the community elegant enough to possess that last word in stoves. But the pride of the pump-master woman's kitchen, and the reason why everybody thought it the finest and classiest in the world, were the various pots and dishes she could boast of. They were all earthenware, but they were richly ornamented with all sorts of fancy designs. On many vessels these designs represented flowers, bees, squirrels, butterflies, antelopes, birds, tigers, lions, dogs, coyotes. Yet of all these flowers, insects, birds, and animals, not one looked natural; they were creations of an Indian artist who was in no way satisfied with the work of the Creator and thought he could do a lot better if he were given the power to create life. Some of these pots were neatly arranged on a shelf, others were hanging in rows against boards nailed to the posts on which the roof rested. Whenever a woman visitor came to see the pump-master woman, she just stood in front of these rows of pots and gazed at them with shining eyes as if she were beholding paradise. All the other families in the settlement used pots and vessels of the crudest sort, most of them broken or cracked. Two families, and the Garcia family was one of them, owned only potsherds. So very high class was the pump-master woman that she actually used these beautiful vessels and did not keep them just for decoration.

The coffee was cooked with crude brown sugar. In another pot black beans were being boiled. A piece of sheet iron about twenty inches square leaned against the wall—to be used to heat tortillas. In a reed basket tied to a piece of rusty wire dangling from a rafter, the tortillas left over from an earlier meal were kept. There were other foodstuffs in that basket. In fact, it was the pantry of the house.

The Garcia had gone once again to her hut. What she was looking for or what she expected to find, she herself would not have been able to say if she were asked. When she returned, carrying the lantern which seemed to have become a part of her, she watched the divers for a few minutes as if they were fishing for something she was not the least interested in. Then she

79

walked with dragging feet, as if in a dream, towards the pump-master's.

Manuel was sitting on a bench, gloomy and brooding. He saw his mother standing beside him. With wide, glassy eyes he stared at her. An idea entered his mind. He jumped up, crossed the bridge, and, along the sandy path which passed through the jungle to distant villages, he walked into the night.

15

   The pump-master was throwing his hook untiringly into the water. Like an expert, he carefully sounded the bottom, trying to get the right feel for the shrubs and for what might be the kid's body. Occasionally he pulled out a load of dripping weeds.

The divers began to show fatigue. Less and less often did they dive, and longer and longer did they hold on to the bridge posts before diving again. A few did not go to the bridge posts at all, but swam or waded to the banks where they could stand on their feet.

The old white-haired man had to give up. Soon all the others swam to the banks, dressed, and went to the fires. Some of them were blue-lipped and had sickly white faces.

The fires, too, seemed tired. No longer did they blaze so lustily. The men and boys who had gone into the bush to get fuel were also tired and were now resting. Gradually the fires died down and soon they were only heaps of embers. The flaming sticks and branches used for torches had turned into black clubs set with sleepy sparks.

One lantern at the pump-master's had burned out. A boy was sent across the bridge to ask the neighbors for kerosene.

Two divers were standing by a fire smoking cigarettes. They were dressed in only a shirt tied round their loins— ready to dive again if somebody asked them to.

Because of all the work in and around the river, many people had in the meantime come to believe the Garcia's story true. Those who refused to believe it did so for no other reason than that they believed that no human being, not even a little boy, could die without any noise. To them death was so great an event that it could not occur silently, safe in bed, from old age. Through their experiences they connected death with much shouting, yelling, swearing, shooting, knifing, clubbing, the falling of a horse, the crash of a tree, the sudden descent of a rock. If one fell into the river or a lake one cried for help. There was always noise when a man died. Therefore they did not believe it possible that death could walk among so many grown-up men and women assembled for a gay dance without a leaf stirring. Death never worked that way! They had searched the river merely to show the sad mother that she must not think herself all alone in the world, that she was surrounded by friends, and that every one of them would willingly sacrifice anything he possessed to bring the kid back.

Someone now had a new idea. Two men searched for a long pole. Having found one, they began sounding the bottom along both sides of the bridge, insisting that if the kid were there they would feel him with a thin flexible pole.

Once more the picture changed entirely.

Around the dying fires, some standing, some squatting, men and boys were talking and smoking. The low fires illuminated them so little that only mere shadows of figures could be seen. Near one fire a heated discussion was going on, but only half sentences and broken incoherent phrases could be heard, though violent and impressive gestures could be seen through the dancing smoke.

A few men and women were sitting on the bridge. Boys were snatching gleaming sticks and branches out of the fires and swinging them through the air to sketch fantastic figures against the black walls of night.

A mouth-organ was being played somewhere. Two girls were singing in a mournful manner from a place hidden behind bushes. From behind the pump-shed the giggling of a young woman was heard, joined by the half-suppressed but animated and eager voice of a man. From another place deep in the darkness of night, there came the harsh voice of a woman quarreling with a man. A gush of light breeze carried a man's voice saying in a hushed tone: "Don't shout; they can hear you," and a woman answered: "Be quiet, you burro." Someone was whistling beyond the camp of the caravan, and his whistling was arrogant and boastful, like that of a man who has just conquered a difficult situation.

On the square in front of the pump-master's, groups were slowly forming again. They talked, but in a rather tired way, because whatever one said or wanted to say had already been said a hundred times before.

Women and girls were walking about or sitting on benches and on piles of logs and rotten sleepers. Many of them went over to the kitchen, where the pump-master woman served them steaming hot coffee in little enameled cups and in small earthen pots. The coffee was black. In each case, when the hostess offered a guest a cup of coffee, she nodded her head in the direction of a sugar bowl. It was meant for those who wanted the coffee sweeter than it was already.

Each woman or girl drank only half a cup and handed the rest to someone else, so that everyone might have at least a few gulps. The night had become still cooler and the hot coffee was welcomed. No guest pushed or jostled to be served first. Everyone awaited his or her turn.

On the bridge several men were still sounding the river in the hope of finding the kid there.

The roosters began to crow for the first time. It was one hour before midnight.

16

 The pump-master had ceased casting his hook into the river. He joined our group and talked of other fatal accidents he had witnessed. The kid was practically forgotten. No one mentioned him any more.

The Garcia was the first to whom hot coffee was offered. She was the guest of honor of the pump-master woman. That meant very much.

In this little settlement hidden in the jungle the pump-master woman was considered more or less the same as a duchess is in a European principality. She could read and also write fairly well. Therefore she was regarded as a highly educated woman. Her children had no lice—at least not as many as the other children had. What is more, her children did not run about naked. The boys wore a pair of ragged pants and the girls a patched-up, cheap, rather flimsy skirt. As for herself, the pump-master woman owned five muslin dresses, all alike in style, but different in color. Furthermore, she possessed five shirts, which she did not call chemises, because she insisted that a shirt is just a shirt and nothing more. Every woman in the

84

settlement knew that she had two blue and two yellow pairs of bloomers and two pink step-ins. Two of the bloomers and one step-in, however, could no longer be really counted. They were worn out. Then she had earrings of genuine gold. She also owned a Spanish comb set with little pearls which looked real, but she was honest enough to admit that they were only of paste and that the little stones in the comb were also false.

Her husband was the owner of a special suit for Sunday—and it included a coat. A suit with a coat, that's the thing—where everybody's suit consists only of a pair of cotton pants.

They had a clock, an alarm clock at that. Furthermore, they had a real mirror, which was framed. For their table they had a knife and two forks, not to mention the spoons, of which they had seven. But the greatest thing they owned was a real mattress, with springs, and a bed made of iron, with big brass knobs at the four corners. Who else in the world, everybody asked, had such a bed and such a mattress? Perhaps the president of the republic.

Of course, the pump-master could afford all that luxury. Wasn't he an employee of the railroad? Railroad employees were the greatest men under heaven. Whatever the pump-master woman said was worth ten times as much as anything the priest said. He who was befriended by the pump-master woman did not need the queen of England, whoever that might be. It is still doubtful that the queen of England owns two pairs of silk stockings, as the pump-master woman does, and whether the queen of England possesses three silk handkerchiefs and one of lace; that would have to be proved before anybody here would believe it. For what people said about the riches of kings and queens and presidents and such gentry, well, it wasn't always true. On the other hand, everything said about the riches and the luxury of the pump-master woman was absolutely true, because everyone had seen it.

While the women were hanging around the pump-master's

kitchen, gossiping and chatting, there was suddenly great excitement in one of the groups. One heard rapid speech interrupted by a flood of questions.

One of these questions finally came to us very clearly: "What did you say? The kid wasn't there?"

The mule-driver and the boy who accompanied him had returned from the nearest village, where they had gone because of the boy who reported that he had seen little Carlos riding in that direction, towards Pacheco.

"No, he wasn't there. And no one has seen him."

"Have you asked everywhere, in all the huts?"

"Of course we have. Everybody was asleep when we arrived. Yet we went to every choza and asked every family we found at home if they had seen the kid. None had."

"Did you also ask if the boy might have passed through the pueblo alone or with somebody, a boy or a youngster?"

"We certainly have. The whole day long no one from Pacheco has come this way and no one who is not of the village has been seen there any time today or tonight. The dogs would have barked if somebody had passed through the pueblo at night."

"Now what about the trail? Have you looked well at the trail?"

"No fresh tracks on the trail, I'm sure. We lighted the trail twenty times and at different sites too. No fresh tracks of any sort of horses or burros or anything save cattle which marched home from the bush and the pastures in the evening. We're absolutely sure that if the kid went away alone or with some other boy he certainly did not go that way. I know all the side trails and the veredas going in other directions off the main trail and we've looked them over too, and very carefully. No tracks on them either."

The muleteer gave the mule he had been riding to a man standing near by, asking him to return it to its owner. Then he walked to his camp, followed by the group which was still asking questions.

The mule-driver noticed the Garcia woman sitting on a bench in the portico. He went to her, for until now she had not known of his return.

She stood up and looked at him, and his eyes immediately began to wander from one to another of the men who had followed him. He could not bear her stare. He wanted to say something. But she sat down again before he opened his mouth. She knew his report. The mule-driver turned his back to her and faced us. He looked as though he were guilty of the kid's disappearance. Not until he had gone far enough away from her and had mixed with the men in the crowd and lighted a cigarette did he feel well again.

Not knowing what else I could do, I went to the bridge, where one Indian was still sounding the bottom. Suddenly he turned to me and said in a low voice: "Señor, I have him. There, touch the stick yourself and you'll feel him all right."

"Be calm, Perez," I said to him; "if you make any noise now, we'll have the whole crowd around in a second and then we can do nothing. Let's be sure first before we say a word. Keep the stick fixed where it is now."

With utmost care I took the pole from his hands. Inch by inch I sounded the bottom, moving the stick lightly. No doubt there was something at the bottom, but it could have been the body of an animal, a pig, or a dog, or a goat. Again I pushed the stick slowly down against whatever it was that was lying on the ground and again I felt that body very distinctly.

"Well," Perez asked, "what do you make of it?"

"I am not so sure yet. We'd better not stir up the people, not yet. We would make ourselves only ridiculous if we howled and afterwards found it was a heap of mud."

I tried to measure the mass, its length and width. So far we had touched only something which might be a chest or a belly.

Sounding to one side I found that the body had no length and nothing I felt could be taken for legs or arms. It was a body with the same extension in every direction. So I was convinced that the thing we had found could be nothing but a thick ball of grass or a pack of accumulated twigs, held together by a few big branches or by lianas. Whatever it was, by no means could it be the body of a boy. Perez admitted his mistake. He dropped the stick and let it lie on the bridge. While I was walking off I looked back and it seemed to me that the pole had taken on an expression of accusation. Perhaps I was only tired. It was near midnight.

I went to the pump-master's, where I was offered hot coffee, black beans, and tortillas. It was now the men's turn to be served.

The bridge was entirely abandoned. Women and girls were chatting gaily. The coffee, it seemed, had given all the visitors fresh energy. All that had occupied their minds during the last three hours was apparently forgotten or at least cast aside for the time being. It was obvious that the weariness of these people who had been on their feet since sunrise was growing and their emotions were getting dull. Even the Garcia was seen to laugh a few times. As the kid had not been found in the river, she tried to convince herself that he had not tumbled in, but that in fact he had ridden to Tlalcozautitlan as the two boys had said and that he would be found in that small town asleep in some nook.

Everyone agreed to wait until Garcia returned from Tlalcozautitlan. If he returned alone, with no news as to the kid's whereabouts, they were all going to stay here the whole night and as soon as morning arrived the river would be searched more thoroughly. Their mood was rapidly returning to normal. If there had been music, they would soon have gone on with the dance.

A few men, tired of standing around and talking about the

same thing over and over again, slowly walked back to the bridge, where they picked up the hook and the long stick and started fishing again, after lighting a fresh torch.

For five minutes the Garcia watched those men on the bridge. Suddenly she yelled and with her lantern swinging in one hand ran to the bridge.

Holding the lantern over the water, leaning forward on tiptoe, she cried wildly: "Chico mio! My little one! Carlos, my darling! Mi nene, mi nene! Come back to your mother, who loves you so dearly! Oh, come back to me, Carlosito! Where are you, chiquitito mio? Carlosito, my sweet little boy!"

The pump-master and another man hurried up to her and grasped her by her arms to prevent her from jumping into the river. She seemed to have lost control of herself. Kicking, pushing the two men away from her, using her feet and arms and even the lantern for defense, she yelled at them: "Let me go! Caray, let me go! What do you want from me? What have I done? Leave me alone, for God's sake or for the devil's, but leave me alone!"

17

 On this side of the river-bank, not far from the end of the bridge, a group of men began to attract attention. There was excited talking, nodding of heads, animated gesticulation. On coming closer I saw that the speaker was the same old white-haired Indian whom I had observed earlier in the night. The group, with that old man in its midst, marched off to the pump-master's.

And once more the bridge became a very lively scene. Boys had broken away from the group after receiving certain instructions and they were now on the bridge preparing something which I could not make out, for I, too, was going to the pump-master's to find out what was happening.

All over the place people began to hustle, scattering in all directions. It was obvious they had a definite purpose in spite of the fact that they looked like ants running around aimlessly. Most of the people, however, did not know the cause of all that liveliness, because it seemed that those in the know had no time to stop and answer questions. People asked one another what was going to come out of that sudden agitation. While no one mentioned it, everybody realized that the kid was the center of the noise and bustle.

The two men who, a little while ago, had started fishing again were now working faster than ever. Two others joined them at this moment.

At the pump-master's choza I heard the old Indian say to the woman: "Yes, señora, a thick candle it must be."

"Sorry; I've only a few thin ones, but you are welcome to them," the pump-master woman answered.

"That won't do." The old Indian looked around and asked: "Who might have a thick candle around here? Does anybody here have a good thick candle?"

"I don't think that anybody has that sort of candle," the woman said; "they are all thin ones, the same as I offered you. Of course, I know they are not of much use, since they bend over so quickly because of the heat."

"If we could only get a good strong candle that would stand, up," the old Indian repeated, looking vaguely around as if he expected such a candle to fall out of the skies.

"Olla, wait a minute," the pump-master woman shouted triumphantly. "I'm sure I've got a good strong candle. It's only," she added in a sad voice, "it's only that this candle is a consecrated one, one specially blessed by the señor cura. I've kept it in the house since the Corpus Christi celebration in Rio Lodoso."

"A consecrated one?" the old Indian gasped. "A consecrated one, a real consecrated one! Woman, be thanked, that's exactly the very one I'm looking for. Now we can't fail. Bring it! Quick! Hurry! Please let me have that candle, señora!"

The pump-master woman took a lantern from the post and disappeared in her hut. The old Indian explained to the men: "A consecrated candle is a thousand times better than any other, no matter how beautiful it may look or how costly it is. But this one, being blessed, will work in no time."

91

He looked around and discovered a wooden case. It was an ordinary box in which canned milk or soap might have been shipped, but it was weather-beaten, so its exact origin could not be made out.

The old man drew the box into the light of the lantern. Carefully looking it over, he finally selected a board which he broke off. It was half an inch thick and perhaps twenty by ten in area.

He pulled out all the nails. Then he balanced it, held it up to the light, and judged its evenness, for, as he explained, all four corners had to be exactly on the same level; if the board were bent even slightly, it would be useless. After looking at it from every angle he said: "This board will do, if any."

The pump-master woman came out of her house holding in her hand a fairly thick candle half burned down and adorned with a little cross of gold paper. It was the sort of candle which the children of the poor carry to their first communion. The children of the rich carry thicker and longer candles, richly decorated to show the Lord and His Virgin Mother, who otherwise might not know that the parents of these children can afford to be more generous—so far as candles are concerned, for in other things it does not matter, because nobody can see it.

Having laid the board on the ground, the old man took the lantern the pump-master woman was holding and put it beside the board. With his fingernails he marked the exact center of the board. Then he lifted it up, put the tip of his forefinger at the marked center, turned the board upside down and balanced it on his forefinger. Satisfied with this test, he again laid the board on the ground.

He lit the candle, allowed a few drops of the hot paraffin to fall on his center mark, placed the candle firmly on these drops, waited a minute, and then touched the candle to see whether it would stand. He worked with great patience and still greater care. From all sides and angles he looked at the candle to be sure that it was standing absolutely straight. "If it were inclined towards one side even only slightly, success would be doubtful," he explained while admiring his job as an artist would.

A score of men and women watched every move the old Indian made. The longer they observed what he was doing, the more they showed an expression of awe in their faces. They might lose all their fear, even all reverence towards their Catholic priests. But they could not lose their deep-rooted fear, reverence, and awe for anybody of their own race who was considered gifted with divine powers and with a knowledge of nature's secrets. If the old man had said: "Now I need the bleeding heart of one of you," half a dozen men and youngsters would have stepped forward to offer it. Not so much out of sheer joy or of a faint hope of becoming saints in the hereafter, but merely because they had lost their own free will and had become spellbound. None of them would offer his heart or even a hand to please a Catholic priest. Their brujos and medicine men still held immense power over their souls and minds—in most cases for their own good.

Everybody knew without asking that all of the old man's strange and mysterious manipulations had something to do with the missing kid. No one spoke. No one interrupted the old man with questions. The more patiently he worked and made his tests, the bigger became the circle of people surrounding him. But they were no longer standing close, in their neighborly intimacy, as they did half an hour ago. The old man was growing into something which made him seem different and difficult for them to comprehend. Everybody was sure that he was trying to get in touch with the beyond on behalf of the child.

He now lifted the board from the ground. As carefully and devotedly as a priest carries the monstrance, he carried the board towards the river-bank. All the people followed as if it were a procession.

Those who were still on the bridge remained there to watch and learn what it was all about. The few who were still fishing with hook and pole also took notice and ceased working. They dropped their tools and came slowly forward.

18

 An old, old Indian woman with a thousand wrinkles in her face, who was surely more than a hundred years of age, was squatting on the bridge. Like all the others, she watched the procession, but she showed little interest, let alone curiosity. She was smoking a thick cigar and puffed away with great gusto. Seeing her calm and philosophic serenity, I realized that it must be a very great thing to be a hundred years old and not an inmate of an institution for the aged, but rather the honored and respected chief of a family or a clan.

After each puff she contemplated her cigar, apparently brooding over the sad fact that everything good on this earth must end sooner or later, even a good cigar. And a good cigar it was, no doubt, because its leaves had not been cooked, cured, toasted, perfumed, cooled, sweetened; and a shipload never coughed as long as you left it alone. From her lack of interest I conceived the idea that besides the old man she was the only one who knew what was going to happen.

I squatted Indian fashion beside her.

"Caray!" I said to her. "That cigar of yours is a good one. It smells like paradise."

"You're telling me, me who made it! And besides, my young man, mind your own goddamned business. Get me?"

It was too late to mind my own goddamned business. I could take it. So I went on: "What are they doing there with that candle on the board?"

She looked at me with half—no, with almost fully closed eyes, and the wrinkles on her face trebled in number. Then, obviously satisfied with my bearing, she blew out a huge cloud of smoke, brooded over the loss of tobacco, and then said: "If you must know, damned gringo, if you must know how we do our things without asking your advice or permission, well, they're searching for that good-for-nothing bastard of that lousy hussy—lazy bitch that she is—and if she had looked in time for her brat and what he was doing, we would not have to look for him now and call heaven and God and the devil for help. Never mind, young man, they will get him all right. Now they will get him out of the dirt and mud, now that at last they're searching the proper way, as they should have done four hours ago and not waited until he is eaten up by the crabs."

"How do you mean, señora, searching the proper way?"

"Searching. Yes, that's what I said, searching. If that brat is in the river and nowhere else, they'll have him in a quarter of an hour, provided there is not much current."

"How can he be in the river, señora? We have searched the river for hours and we have not found him."

She grinned at me ironically. Her teeth were thick, large, and of a brownish-yellow color. The gums had retreated so far that her teeth were laid bare to the roots, which made them look even longer. "What did you say? Oh yes, you said you searched for hours. What people call searching in these days, that's what you have done and nothing better. How smart and

96

clever you are, all you people of today! Talking of superstition and never knowing a goddamned thing about what is behind the world you see with your eyes—or you think you see while in fact you see nothing because you are blind and deaf and dumb and you can't even smell. That's the trouble you people suffer from. The way you and the others have been searching, well, my young man, you may be sure that you could search that way for seven days and you wouldn't find the brat if he didn't come up by himself. If you had waited until the morrow, there wouldn't have been much of him left to show his father, that damned drunkard, when he comes back from that useless trip which anyway he made only to get booze. Every sane person knows that the little devil is in the river and nowhere else. The trouble is, there is not one single sane person around, myself not excluded, because I am just as mad and crazy as all the others. I tell you, my young man, they are all crazy here, waiting for the music to come and none realizing that the music has been here and playing for hours already. But they are deaf and blind, that's what they are."

"I think you are right, señora. Only you see I can't understand the meaning of that board with the candle on it. We have looked and searched with torches and huge bonfires for light. If we couldn't find him with so much light, how do they expect to find him with that little candle?"

"Borregos, yes, that's what you are, muttonheads. You and your iron hooks and poles and sticks and lanterns, which are good for a dog but not for a human. The candle alone will find him as surely as it's night now and there'll be day tomorrow. All the old man has to do is watch where the candle goes, and wherever it stops, there below is the kid."

"How can the candle find him if we didn't?"

She puffed her cigar, blew out huge clouds, contemplated the cigar with dreamy eyes, and then scanned me all over from top to bottom to see whether I was worthy of being talked to any longer. It had all come out in bits which I had had to arrange in the right order myself to catch what she wanted to say. That was difficult because she mixed words of the Indian idioma with her poor Spanish. But she accompanied her words with vivid facial expressions and with an occasional gesture, so it was not so hard after all to understand her. Her eyes often opened wide and then they would sparkle like those of a young woman telling her intimate girl friend of her honeymoon experiences.

All my attention was now concentrated upon the activities at the river-bank. I forgot to ask the old woman more questions, but I was aware that she was watching me, catlike, to learn what I might think of the strange performance I was witnessing. I was sure she was taking note of every move or gesture I made. No doubt I was gaining her confidence every minute. The fact is I was taking the whole rite, or whatever it was, very seriously; I would under no circumstances make fun of it or joke about it. After all, every religion is right and proselytism is always wrong.

On the bank, a score of men were again forming a circle around the old Indian. He held the board with the candle on it before him. The flame of the candle was on a level with his eyes. I think the old Indian priests of the ancient Aztecs and Toltecs must have looked as he did at that moment if one forgot his simple peasant clothes. About him there was the dignity and the aloofness of the high priest who is about to celebrate a mysterious rite. Perhaps he would evoke the gods whom he knew and recognized in his heart, for the Lord to whom he and everyone of his race prayed in church dwelled on their lips only and never reached their hearts.

From the corners of my eyes I saw that the old woman did not cease watching me. And still I had no reason to disapprove of what those men were doing. It was their business, not mine.

The old woman, guessing correctly what I was going to ask her, suddenly said: "The kid is calling all the time. Can't you hear it?"

Perhaps I dreamed those words. Yet there they were. Rather dazedly I said: "I am sorry, señora, I can't hear him calling. Did you say the kid is calling?"

"That's exactly what I just said. And you don't have to be sorry that you can't hear him calling. I can't hear it either, the way we hear ordinary things. No human ear can hear him calling the ordinary way. It is the light of the candle which is hearing his calls. We can only watch and see the calling, but not hear it ourselves."

"The light of the candle? Did you say the light of the candle?" I was still not sure that I wasn't dreaming. Or perhaps I did not really understand what the old woman was saying in her corrupt Spanish mixed with Indian lingo. So I asked once more: "Do you really mean to say the light hears the kid calling?"

"Yes, and don't make me believe you are too dumb to understand plain language. I'll tell you something else. So far no one knows if the kid is actually in the river. But if he is, and I am sure he is, then he'll call the light close to him. The light will follow his calling and it will come to him as sure as there is a God in heaven. And the light will stand by because the light has to obey his calls and it cannot do anything on its own account or of its own free will. Not in such a case."

It was night. It was a pitch-black night. It happened in a tropical jungle. I was in the midst of Indians, very few of whom I knew, and even those few I knew only superficially. What was it the old woman had just told me? What she had told me was something out of their everyday life, an ordinary thing. I wondered which of us was mad. One of us surely was. Anyway, in such a night, in a jungle, among Indians, whatever else the old woman might have told me would have sounded unnatural. The old woman simply could not talk any other way than she did. It was in harmony with everything. I saw clearly what the men were doing on the river-bank, so it could not be a dream. I was awake. And I remained squatting beside the old woman. She spoke no more, enjoyed her cigar immensely, and with a bored look in her eyes she watched the group of men preparing the mysterious ceremony.

The old Indian began to speak in a loud, chanting voice. What he said I could not understand, because I was still on the bridge.

Now he ceased speaking and moved the board before him three times up and down and three times sidewise and then once more up and down. After a short silence he raised his voice and again chanted a few lines. This time his chant was taken up by a dozen of the men standing around him and they repeated these lines as a kind of response.

All the men had taken off their hats. Everybody near followed the ceremony with solemn zest.

I leaned forward to try to catch the words, for I would have liked to know them. But I preferred to stay away even if I had to miss the words. Theirs was a religious service to which I had not been invited, so I considered it rude to go close when everyone was aware of the fact that I was not moved by faith, but by curiosity.

I could pick up some phrases. I learned that in the main it was Spanish they spoke. Yet this Spanish of theirs was blended with words and phrases taken from the Indian idioma, which was still spoken by hundreds of families in that jungle region. However, the expression "Madre Santisima!" was used so frequently that it stood out clearly. I felt, however, that they prayed to the Most Holy Virgin only with their lips while with their hearts they were calling upon their ancient holy mother, perhaps to Cioacoatl.

This ceremony lasted about ten minutes. The old Indian

100

raised the board high above his head. The light of the candle was reflected in the water. While holding the board in this position, he chanted a few lines more. The audience joined him before he ended. And they all finished together. I listened carefully, but there was no Amen, only a sound like an owl's hoo-oo.

Quick as a flash Perez stripped. He stood in the water for a while. Then with arms stretched forward he strode slowly towards the old Indian, who also came forward until he too was standing in the water. With a solemn gesture he handed Perez the board and mumbled a few words. Perez gestured with his right hand over his chest and then over the board. Perhaps it was the sign of the cross that he made—perhaps another sign. When he received the board he also said a few words in a low voice as a response to the old man's chant. As soon as the board was in Perez's hands, the old Indian made similar gestures with his right hand over the board and then over his heart. After this he stepped back to the bank, walking backwards with his face to the board.

Perez carried the board high above his head. He waded into the river until the water reached his chest. Now he stopped and waited until the water had calmed down again. Then he set the board upon the water with infinite care. When the board was floating he waded slowly back to the river-bank, facing the strange little raft as he did so.

19

 The board rests quietly on the water as if it were deciding which way to go.

Perez wraps his shirt around his loins and steps back from the river-bank. With his eyes fixed upon the board he keeps walking backward, then turns to the bridge, from where he can see better what is happening. As I was told later, the board might go straight to its goal, but it might also merely wobble, and in that case the right direction could be determined only by an expert.

All the people present are spellbound. For moments on end they forget to breathe and then have to catch up suddenly, so that a ceaseless moaning comes from their lips. They seem to force themselves not to wink and their eyes redden and widen, which gives the crowd the appearance of being in a deep trance.

Some men hold their hats in their hands; others have thrown theirs away. Nobody smokes any more. Not a word is heard, not even a murmur or a whisper. Only the singing, chirping, and fiddling of the jungle fills the night. This great jungle symphony is at times unexpectedly interrupted by a deep silence, as if the jungle insects were ordered to stop for two or three seconds, for no other reason than to break out again louder and more intensely than before. These sudden intervals in the jungle music deepen the mystery of the night and heighten the tension of the people who are waiting almost ecstatically for the miracle to happen. No one knows whether the miracle will take place tonight as it took place, according to their traditions, five hundred, yes, ten thousand years back under similar circumstances. All present have a faith which no power could shake. There is not one in the whole crowd who even for a second thinks the light could fail to obey the call of the lost boy. Of course, it would fail if the kid is not in the river, for then he could not call, and the light has no will of its own; it can only go if it is called. It will float down the river and disappear if the boy is not in the water.

Suddenly that multi-headed body utters a cry and takes a deep breath as though there were only two very huge lungs in that body.

The board has started to move.

With infinite slowness it begins to sail away from the bank towards the middle of the river. Now it stops, wobbles, sways, trembles slightly. Then it takes again the same direction.

The bridge is crowded with people. Those along the rim are kneeling, tightly pressed against each other, their heads reaching as far over the edge as possible. With burning eyes they stare at the slowly moving board. Nobody breathes more than absolutely necessary, partly because of tension, but more because their breathing might throw the board off its course.

I stand on the bank near the end of the bridge, from which point I can see the face of everyone kneeling along the rim. This row of eager faces is lighted by the new bonfires on the banks. The fact is I am far more interested in these sixty or seventy faces and in these bronze and dark-yellow bodies than in what the board is doing at this moment. The board I am sure will do its job all right. If it does not, it will be of little concern to me. Yet during the rest of my life I may never again behold such a grandiose picture, such a huge human body with threescore and more heads, all thinking the same thought, all concentrated upon the same hope, all charmed by the little flame of an ordinary candle. Their deep brown eyes reflect that little flame as if each contained a tiny, forlorn star. There are half-naked bodies, stark naked bodies, bodies clothed in rags only, and bodies covered with white shirts and white or yellow cotton pants. So thick is their black wiry hair that it looks as if these men had heavy fur caps on their heads.

Against the simple and natural clothes of the men the women's dresses from modern sweat-shops make a pitiful contrast. What sin have these women committed that providence could allow Syrian jobbers to hang upon those beautiful bodies dresses designed by immigrant watch-repairers starving in New York's East Side? In their simple week-day skirts, even in their rags, these women are in harmony with the jungle, the river, the bridge, the asthmatic pump, the pack train, the alligators, the earth, the whole universe. Now they are aniline-dyed ghosts, foul bastards of the land, nobody's daughters. Thanks to a merciful God and to Nature with its eternal good taste, beautiful wild flowers still grow and blossom in jungle and bush, and these women can pick them at their hearts' desire and with them cover the ugliness of modern products. And it is only on account of the wild flowers and orchids of the jungle that these women do not lose all their contact with the earth which has borne them.

The mysterious performance of which I am a witness, the crowd's belief that the miracle will happen, the dim light of the lanterns in the pump-master's portico, the licking flames of the bonfires, the torches held by boys on the bridge, the floating board with the lighted candle in the river, that huge

104

body of excited beings who are not my race, at this moment breathing as one, their eyes gazing without winking and each with a tiny star in it, the gloomy silence of that mass of men, the never ceasing whining of the jungle—all this depresses me and makes my heart heavy. My throat is parched. My tongue feels as though it were wood. Where is the world? Where is the earth on which I used to live? It has disappeared. Where has mankind gone? I am alone. There is not even a heaven above me. Only blackness. I am on another planet, from which I never can return to my own people. I shall never again see green meadows, never again the waves of wheat fields, never again shall I wander through the forests and around the lakes of Wisconsin, never again shall I ride over the plains of Texas and breathe the air of desolate goat ranches. I cannot come back to the earth, my true mother, and never shall I see the sun rise. I am with creatures I do not know, who do not speak my language, and whose souls and minds I can never fathom. One, only one out of this crowd has to stand up at this moment, only one has to point his finger at me and yell: "Look at that man! Look at him! He is the white, who has not been invited to come here, but he came nevertheless. He is the guilty one. By his blue eyes and by his skin of the pale dead he has brought the wrath of our gods upon us poor people. He is a gringo. He has brought us misfortune and sorrows. He has come only yesterday and today our little boy had to leave us, driven away by that white man and making the kid's mother weep like the skies in the rainy season. He has been here only two days and the river, which hates him, has robbed us of our beloved little child. Look at his eyes and you will see that with those eyes he is poisoning our children and bewitching all of us!"

If I never come back again, if I am sacrificed here and now, tonight, nobody, no consul, no ambassador, no government, will ever know what has become of me and where my bones are bleaching under the sun. The buzzards won't leave anything of me that could be identified. "Disappeared on a trip through the jungle." Or perhaps: "Caught by alligators on a fishing trip in swampy territory." This will be the last the old folks at home will hear of me.

Why do I feel uncomfortable? There, only a few yards away, there stands Sleigh, my fellow citizen, white of color like myself, thoughts the same as mine, brought up in the same traditions, speaking the same language. He is standing behind the men who are kneeling on the bridge, and he too has his eyes fixed upon the board slowly floating on the river. Suppose this crowd, stirred up by somebody gone mad, were to jump at me to make me pay for the lost kid, Sleigh would be my guardian angel, my life-saver; he would protect me with his very body. Certainly. Most certainly. Because he is my fellow citizen, singing with me the *Star-Spangled Banner*. He would save me. He would cock his hat slightly, with a lazy gesture, and he would say: "Why, now, see here, you folks, you can't do that. That is stupid. He didn't throw the kid in the river. I'm plumb sure he didn't. He is a mighty good fellow and nobody can deny that." Having said this, he would turn to me and say: "You must excuse me, I've got to look after that goddamned cow. Christ, if I only knew where to find that damn bitch. Perhaps she has come home at last. I'll go and see." So he would go and leave me alone with that frenzied mob. After I have been torn to pieces he would return and talk to the neighbors, telling them that the cow has not come home yet and that surely a pair of tigers or lions must be roaming in the vicinity. Then, on seeing the last ragged shreds of me, he would say: "Well, you men, you shouldn't have done that. It isn't right. I told you so before. Anyhow, who would have thought that of him? He seemed to be a fine chap. I don't think he threw the kid into the river. You shouldn't have done that. Well, well, who would have thought such a thing of him?"

106

Sleigh. Who is Sleigh? What is he to me? He was born in the same God's great country I was. Nevertheless he is farther away from me than our president. Sleigh. He has lived more than half his life among these Indians. He is married to an Indian woman. His children don't speak one word of American, they know only Spanish and quite a few phrases of the Indian idioma. Sleigh. The meals he eats are Indian, and he eats as the Indians do, without using a fork, shoveling up his meat, beans, and gravy with a torn-off bit of tortilla, wrapping the whole thing up and pushing it into his wide-open mouth, swallowing the food and eating the tortilla-made spoon simultaneously. He lives in an Indian jacal on an earthen floor under a grass roof. He would feel most uncomfortable in a house or a bungalow. Without moving an eyelash he would stand by and look on should this crowd become infuriated and hammer me into a pulp. I am absolutely alone among these people. And I also know perfectly well that whatever might happen to me, no battle-cruiser will steam into this jungle with a crew yelling: "Hip, hip, hi! Everything is under control, we have the situation well in hand!" It is a very good thing to know that. One thus becomes a fatalist. The more fatalistic I become, the closer I get to understanding these people. They could not bear life were they not all fatalists.

20

  The board is some fifteen feet from the river-bank. It stops for half a minute. Now it begins to whirl slowly and, still whirling, drifts farther towards the middle of the river, gradually nearing the slow current. For five feet or so it moves along that current. Then it stops again. And again it whirls as if it were trying to get out of the stream.

After a few minutes it again follows the current for a short distance. Then it stops abruptly. It begins whirling again. At first it does so very slowly, then quicker and quicker still, and at the same time it starts moving back towards the bridge and now, as can be clearly seen, it moves contrary to the current. I personally cannot see any miracle in that, because all rivers have currents of two or more different directions, although usually only for short stretches.

Nor does the crowd regard it as something miraculous or even strange that the board is moving against the current. Only they have a different reason for being calm about it. To them it is something long anticipated. It convinces everybody that the kid is in the river, that he is calling the light, and so the light has to answer his call. Further, it is proof that the body has not been washed downstream.

Which of us, the crowd or I, will be right in the end?

The board floats towards the bridge. It sails so slowly that its movements can be judged only by watching the candle against a fixed mark on the opposite bank.

Now it stops and wobbles on the surface. Apparently it has been caught by a plant or a shrub in the water. That at least is my explanation. Strange as it may seem, the board struggles to free itself.

The crowd is watching that struggle with more tension and excitement than they would a cockfight. Many faces show disappointment. One young man gets ready to wade into the river and help the board out of the tangle. The old Indian commands him to leave the board alone. "No shrub, no branch, nothing that grows or lives in the water can keep the board from going where it has to go. Mind that, muchacho," he counsels him.

The old Indian has told the truth. A few minutes after he spoke the board wobbles faster, begins to whirl, twists itself out of the entanglement. Slowly it sails nearer to the bridge.

It now has reached the bridge and here it touches the seventh post. That post repulses it and, while keeping directly under the rim, it wanders towards the sixth post, where it stops for several minutes.

"There, now it's stopping for good! There is the boy! That's the sign!" A score of men are shouting excitedly.

"Hold it! Hold it!" the old Indian cries. "Go easy, you folks. Let's wait and see first before we make any mistake and stir up the water and lose our best chance. The light is not perfectly quiet yet. I'll give you the word!"

Hardly has he said that when the board starts wriggling. It moves away from the sixth post and sails, whirling all the while, towards the fifth post, still remaining under the rim of

109

the bridge. On the way it is caught by the slight current and carried out for a foot or so. But each time it pulls itself out of the current and struggles back under the rim as though forced to do so by some strong power.

It has reached the fifth post. It hangs on for a few minutes. Then, still clinging to the post, it moves around and sails away from it straight under the bridge for about one and a half feet.

The people kneeling on the rim lean far over and stick their heads under it to watch the board's movements. Everyone in the crowd now thinks himself very stupid for not having fished for the kid under the bridge instead of only along its edge. Several men crawl over to the upstream side of the bridge and put their heads down there. Others lie flat on the planks and watch the miracle through the joints and knot-holes.

The board in the meanwhile has wandered farther under the bridge, but always in a right angle to the fifth post. Now it is under the middle of the bridge. From here it sails towards the fourth post, though only for about a foot.

And here it stops as if it were nailed to the water. It does not mind the current nor the light breeze that sweeps softly across the surface of the river. The manner in which the board has halted is entirely different from that in which it stopped before. Now and then it trembles slightly, as if something were breathing against it from below. But it no longer whirls.

In fact, its behavior is so clear, so definite, that nobody can doubt any longer that the board has found its final destination.

A long-drawn-out groan comes from the crowd as if from one mouth. A hundred heavy sighs fill the air and almost drown out the million voices of the jungle. Many men and women seem covered with thick pearly sweat, while the sweat runs in streams down the faces and bodies of the others. No one bothers to wipe it off. Here and there whispered words float through the night.

110

The board begins softly to dance as if impatient. It seems that it wants to be relieved of its torture. It wriggles, swings about itself, though it does not move as much as two inches. One might think it is trying to go down to the bottom.

The old Indian watches the board like a hawk watching a mouse. He has an infinite calmness of manner. Four or five minutes more he waits, and now he gives the long-expected signal. "There, you may dive now. There is the little one. He is in the river all right. Poor mother, may God save and bless her!" He goes a few paces nearer the bridge.

It is a spot nobody has thought of. Who would have thought that a boy who has tumbled over the rim should be looked for under the middle of the bridge? It seems impossible.

Perez is already in the river. Two men follow him. He is the first on the spot. He pushes the board gently aside so as to have room to dive.

Only a few seconds he is under the water, then he comes up, spits, and says in a thick, sad voice: "He is there! The kid is there! I've touched his little body."

The people on the bridge look at Perez. He has swum to the fifth post, to which he clings with one hand while with the other he wipes from his face the water dripping down from his hair. His face, dimly lighted by the flickering bonfires on the banks, shows an expression of horror mixed with mental pain. He looks up to the bridge and lets his eyes wander over the whole crowd. Everybody knows that he is looking for the Garcia woman, yet none calls her.

At this moment, coming from nowhere at all, the Garcia walks with heavy dragging feet along the bridge to where Perez clings to the post. Everybody steps back to let the woman pass freely. She has heard Perez. Her mouth is wide open. She wants to yell, perhaps she even thinks that she is yelling. But somehow she cannot do so, because her throat is tight as if in a cramp. She raises one hand, makes a fist, and

111

stuffs that fist into her open mouth as deep as it will go. Horror haunts her eyes. Fear flutters over her face with jumping shadows as if huge unseen birds were flying around her. She is trembling with fear of the final sentence. She wishes to hold fast to the last little bit of hope and doubt. Perhaps Perez has erred. Perhaps he has felt only a pack of balled grass. Would to Almighty God that he has erred as have all others before him! Her eyes are slowly moving upwards to heaven. Yet half-way she turns them into the direction of Tlalcozautitlan, where her husband has ridden and where her last glimmer of hope now rests. The kid has surely gone to Tlalcozautitlan with that boy on the white horse. It must be so or the world cannot be right and there can be no God in heaven.

Nobody says a word. Only a shuffling of feet on the bridge is heard. And the singing of the jungle.

Perez has dived again, accompanied by one of the other two men. Soon both come up, their hands filled with wet and rotten shrubs and branches and twigs all dripping with water. They push them away, and down again the two men go.

Bubbles boil on the surface. Torn water plants, branches, bits of shrubs rise and float on the water. One of the two men comes up. One cannot see who he is because only part of his face is visible and that is covered with his matted, dripping hair.

A few seconds later something black is seen rising to the surface. It comes up slowly until it can be identified as the thick hair of Perez. Now his head is fully out. He shakes it as a dog shakes his pelt to free it of water. He blows, breathes heavily, swallows, and rises farther, treading the water with all his power. He is not using his arms this time. In his arms he holds the little Carlosito, whose knees are seen before anything else. His knees protrude high above the rest of his body because they are bent in an unnatural angle so that the heels are only a few inches away from the small of his back. One

112

might think that the kid had been sitting on his heels all during the time he was on the bottom.

Strange. The new American shoes on his little feet draw everybody's first look in a verily obtrusive and arrogant manner, as if they were the most important part of the whole body.

Perez does not look up to the bridge. Partly swimming, partly wading, he makes for the bank.

"Chiquito mio! My baby!" the Garcia yells. She darts to the bank and awaits Perez.

Perez walks up the low slope of the bank. Entirely naked he now stands before the young mother. Still in her cheap sea-green gauze dance dress, with fire-red wild flowers in her hair, on her breast, and in her girdle, she receives Perez with arms stretched out towards the little burden he is carrying.

With an indescribable nobility and solemnity, and in his eyes that pitiful sad look which only animals and primitive people possess, he steps slowly forward. And Perez, the man whose daily task it is to fell the hard trees of the jungle and convert them into charcoal, lays that little water-soaked body in the outstretched arms of the mother with a tenderness that makes one think of glass so thin and fragile that a single soft breath could break it.

21

 At this moment many women uttered a shrill, plaintive wail full of reproach.

That wail, which pierced the blackness of the night as if it meant to break through and rise to the sun in the sky, swelled until all the women fell in. Then it sank and became a low moan. The women wrapped a piece of cloth, be it a rebozo, a black veil, or a shawl, around their heads. Their faces hidden, they wept bitterly.

It was no longer only the death of the Garcia woman's child that they bewailed. By his untimely death the little boy had become every mother's baby. Only a mother knows how a mother feels. No one else, not even God in heaven with all His immaculate wisdom, with all His stern serenity, can feel as a mother does when her baby has been taken away from her.

The Garcia held her baby in her left arm against her breast. With her right hand she squeezed his wet and already shriveled little hands.

Perez stole away from her. He no longer wished to be seen by her, as though he were guilty of an unforgivable crime.

A middle-aged Indian walked up to the mother, bowed his

114

head, and spoke to her. She handed him the little body; he received it very gently. Then he stepped back a few paces. Resolutely and unsentimentally, like an old country doctor, he now grasped the kid firmly by his feet and held him up with the head hanging perpendicularly. He shook the body several times. Only watery blood dripped out of the kid's mouth.

The body was already stiff. In spite of the weight of the body hanging by its feet, the knee joints stretched very little.

While the kid still hung upside down, a thick bruise became visible on the forehead above the left eyebrow. The nose and mouth were swollen and the upper jaw was partly smashed in.

I went near and lifted his head slightly because I wished to see his eyes by the light of a lantern. Holding his head in the palm of my hand, I felt, with the tip of my middle finger, a little hole in the back of his skull. I turned the head round to the light, and from its size I decided that this hole was caused by a fairly thick nail.

The Indian who was holding the body by its feet winked at another man. This man pressed the little body between his hands, moving from the belly down to the chest inch by inch. Even then surprisingly little water came out of the kid's mouth. Yet there was still that trickling of thin blood.

Huge pearls of tears formed in the eyes of the mother, and when her eyes could not hold them any longer, they tumbled down, running down her cheekbones, over the corners of her mouth, down her chin, finally dropping upon her breast. They fell upon the flowers she had fastened on her dress slightly above her heart.

She snorted as though pushed from the inside of her chest, and through her nostrils she blew violently a loud hiss which, it seemed, she had suppressed for hours and which now at last was released in a second. Her nose was running. She looked around vaguely. Then she looked down along her own body, lifted up her green dance dress, and blew her nose in it.

It pained her to see her baby hanging head down, almost like

115

a slaughtered goat. She stared at this lifeless body and, obviously thinking it might hurt him to hang that way for so long a time, she took his head and lifted it. Her eyes fell upon his bent knees. She let the head go and tried to press the joints into a more natural position. While doing so, she blew her nose several times in the folds of her dress and in her sleeves. Again and again she worked at his knees, which would not stretch. Despite her grief she was already thinking of the beautiful ceremony of laying out the body for the funeral. The body had to be presented to the mourners and visitors before being buried. For this occasion it had to be pretty. It was the last thing she could do for her baby, for she did not want him to go to heaven looking like a pauper.

The man who had tried to press the water out of the body understood the mother's desire and made it his job to straighten the knees. By pulling, massaging, kneading, pressing the joints between his labor-hardened hands, he achieved some success at least. While he was working at the knees the mother gently stroked the new shoes on the kid's feet. These shoes had still preserved, in spots, their original brilliance. She pressed the little shoes, caressed them as if they were part of his body, because she remembered how much he liked them. And while she caressed them she doubtless wondered about the mysterious ways of destiny, that this token of brotherly love should have become the cause of the kid's destruction. Overwhelmed by these thoughts she forgot to breathe and her suppressed weeping now almost suffocated her. She tried to gasp for fresh air, opened her mouth wide to let the air in, but instead she yelled so fiercely that it seemed the night of the jungle would be rent into pieces by the scream of a wounded mother accusing the universe of injustice.

There followed a few seconds of silence during which time the world seemed to vanish. Again the mother yelled.

The men standing by felt depressed and shy. They dropped their eyes and fumbled with their hands as little children do

116

when they are ashamed. In the face of the mother's distress the men became little, worthless, poor, and empty in their souls. None dared touch her, none consoled her for fear of doing the wrong thing.

The pump-master woman came up, and without saying one word she embraced the mother as if she meant to crush her ribs. She covered her face with kisses, kissed away her rolling tears. She lifted up her own Sunday dress and with it she dried the mother's tears and wiped her nose. Then she kissed her again and again. The two women wept and sobbed together so that it could be heard all over the wide square.

Who would ever have thought that the pump-master woman, that very proud woman, as highly respected as if she were the president's wife, that this haughty woman could let herself go that way and lose all her composure. The mothers. The mothers. That's what mothers are like. They understand each other when one of them is grieved.

The men felt themselves getting still smaller and poorer on seeing those two women weep together as one. More and more did they feel ashamed of—they did not know what. They had only one wish at this moment, the wish to be able to weep as these two mothers wept. How they envied the two who had busied themselves with the little body!

Sleigh came up. He touched the kid, ran his hand up and down the whole body, and finally said: "He's a goner all right, and I'll go and make coffee. The Garcia woman certainly will like to have something hot in her belly."

The pump-master woman wormed herself very gently out of the Garcia woman's arms and looked at the kid, who was still hanging head down while the two men worked on him. She lifted his head, stroked back his wet hair, and softly patted his cheeks. The watery blood trickled over her hand. With her dress she cleaned his bleeding mouth and blood-smeared nose. The blood still trickled forth.

The kid wore not only new shoes but also new socks, which,

like the shoes, were the first he had ever worn and which were also a gift from his big brother. His short pants, reaching only to his knees, were worn out, patched in a dozen places, and still full of holes. He had no suspenders. Instead he wore a string fastened to one button in front, running across one shoulder, and tied to one button at the back of his pants. The upper part of his body was covered with a torn white cotton shirt which was already too small for him.

While the man holding the body by the feet shook the kid once more in the hope that at last the water would come out, a little wooden whistle fell out of one of the pants pockets. Before it reached the ground his mother caught it. She stared at it and began to weep in a soft and woeful manner. She wiped the tears off her face to have another look at the whistle, then she hid it in the bosom of her dress.

"Didn't he have a hat?" one man asked.

The men who had heard this question got excited. A job was at hand. They could now do something useful. They could jump into the water and fish for the kid's hat.

This hope, though, vanished quickly. If there had been a hat it would have been seen and found long ago or it would have drifted off downstream.

Then the Garcia said that the hat was in the hut, and that this was what had made her doubt that the kid had ridden away, because he would have taken his hat along, for he would have needed it badly on the return trip in the daytime when the sun is high and hot. Half of what she said one had to guess because her speech was constantly interrupted by her blubberings.

We were still standing on the bank not far away from the bridge. Someone was holding up a lantern, and by its light this part of the bridge could be seen clearly. I was looking up, thinking of Sleigh, who had said—it seemed to me a week ago—that he was going to make coffee for somebody. I saw

118

something walking on the bridge towards us. That something was walking slowly and heavily, like a very old man. If it lifted a foot it did so as if it were nailed to the planks and had to be torn off by force. Its head was bent deep upon its breast. Before I saw the face I recognized that strange something by the Texas sombrero it was wearing: Manuel.

He had now reached this end of the bridge. For almost a minute he remained standing there. Then he came up to us without lifting his head. He was pale, as pale as the brown color of his skin would allow. His face had become very small and narrow. Were it not for the hat, I might not have known for a long while who he was, so much had he changed. His eyes were dull and glassy as if they had lost their light.

The Garcia stared at her big stepson. Her eyes were filled with balls of water. She opened her mouth to say something. But the lips closed slowly and stayed closed.

Manuel was now standing by the two men who were holding the kid. They looked at him as if he were a ghost.

It was obvious that he did not wish to see anything. He stretched out his arms, while his head remained hanging. And in his outstretched arms the little brother was gently laid.

No word was spoken. The men and boys who had put their hats on took them off once more while this ceremony of handing the kid to his brother went on.

For a few minutes Manuel stood thus, statue-like, holding the kid in his arms as if he were offering the kid as a sacrifice to the gods. He was the only one with his hat on. It was this wide-brimmed sombrero on his mournfully bowed head, hiding his face, that made this simple act appear like a mysterious rite.

The whole incident became unbearable to me. I was caught by the same fear I had felt for a minute or two while the board was floating upon the water. Any second I expected to see all eyes fixed upon me as having been found guilty of magic or

119

witchcraft and so responsible for the misfortune which had befallen that poor settlement of peaceful natives.

Not so much to help but merely to keep my nerves from going to pieces, I assured myself that I was still alive and sane and healthy by forcing myself to act—even though my action might have drawn everybody's attention to me and perhaps caused the very thing I was afraid of. At the very moment that Manuel was about to turn around to carry the little body to his home, I stepped quickly forward, touched Manuel's arm, and said: "Por favor, amigo, one moment only."

Whether Manuel had heard what I had said I did not know, but he remained standing. I put my hand on the kid's chest, pushed his shirt away, and put my ear above his heart. For a long time I had known that the kid was dead, or at least unconscious and nearly dead, before he reached the water and that he was surely dead five minutes after I had heard the splash. No, after I had heard a fish jumping high into the air to catch a mouthful of mosquitoes. That splash had been caused by a fish. I would swear it was a fish. And I would stick to that story until the end of my life. I did not wish to be haunted all my life by the sound of the splash I had heard early that night.

As I was saying, five minutes after that fish had made a heavy splash the kid was dead and beyond help. There was the bruise over his left eye, there was the little hole in his skull, and there was the smashed upper jaw. He was dead long before he was missed by his mother.

The little body which I touched with my ear was as cold as ice. There was not the faintest throb of that little heart which only five hours ago had been beating so happily. No one here had expected me to declare that the kid was still alive. Yet they let me do as I liked. I lifted the head. Everybody looked at me with a question in his eyes. As though I had not been absolutely sure of my first examination I laid my ear on the clammy chest once more. This time I listened longer and more attentively. I felt the repugnant coldness of death only that much more, and only that much more did I realize the helplessness of man against death. When I raised my head I did not look up; instead I turned away from the crowd, which, I knew without seeing, had their eyes fixed upon me, obviously expecting to hear me promise a miracle. But my silent turning away convinced everybody that no miracle, not even something unexpected, would happen.

My fear had gone. That painful agony which had gripped me twice that night had disappeared entirely. By my careful examination of the kid's heart, useless though it was, I had shown that I was willing to help. So I had been accepted as one of the mourners.

22

 Manuel, with the kid resting in his outstretched arms, marched slowly across the bridge in time to the unheard strains of some funeral hymn.

The mother walked beside him, leaning against the shoulder of a woman who had put one arm around her neck. Both were sobbing.

Behind them the men marched, hat in hand, followed by the women.

On reaching the point on the bridge from which it was supposed the kid had tumbled over, Manuel stopped for half a minute. As his head was still bowed, it could not be seen whether he said a prayer or whispered: "Behold, O Lord, what you have done!"

The Garcia screamed horribly. The woman by her side put both her arms around the mother and talked to her in a low, soft voice. One man stepped to the edge of the bridge and with a few heavy strokes of his machete cut a cross in the rim as a sort of monument.

The procession marched on, arrived at the opposite bank,

122

reached the opening where the settlement was located, and came to a halt at the clean-swept front yard of the Garcia's hut, where in the early evening old man Garcia had been fiddling and Carlosito had had a boxing match with his big brother Manuelito.

Following Manuel and the two women, we entered the hut.

This home proved to be one of the poorest I had ever seen. No table, no chair, no bench, no cot, no furniture of any sort, not even of the cheapest kind. Save a box, there was absolutely nothing which could be used as furniture. In the farthest corner four posts were stuck in the earthen floor. On these four posts there rested a network of thin sticks interwoven and held together by vines and lianas from the jungle. On this flimsy construction there was an old, threadbare blanket and an armful of prairie grass which was used as a pillow. That simple thing was the bed of Garcia and his wife. The kid's bed was a petate, a bast mat, spread out on the earthen floor and now shoved under the bed. Frequently, though, the kid had slept on the grass roof with a ragged piece of cloth for a blanket. His mother had always been afraid that a scorpion would sting him, but he had not minded, preferring the roof for a reason he had been unable to explain.

Several women had hurried to the hut before Manuel and all the others. These women had brought candles, put them into empty beer-bottles loaned by the pump-master, and set them on boxes which had also been obtained from the maestro maquinista. Owing to these preparations, the hut had a solemn aspect which, when the Garcia entered and observed it, caused her to break out crying again.

This time, however, she shook off her despair quickly and resolutely. She found herself confronted now with the tasks of a hostess, let alone her duty to prepare the funeral for her baby. The many obligations she faced helped her to forget her grief. And it was surely a very good thing that she had to get

123

busy around her household. It would save her from becoming morose perhaps for the rest of her life. It is the first twelve hours that count. If one can survive them and keep one's reason under control during this time, one can find life worth while again in a few weeks.

At first she did not know what to do and where to begin. In the machinery of her daily life a very important bolt had been broken and she had to find a substitute for it before that machinery would run perfectly again. So far she knew only that she had to be busy and work hard for the next ten hours. She began with pushing the boxes to places other than where they had been put by the women who had brought them. Each box was moved and all the candles were taken out of the bottles and stuck into others and then the bottles themselves were moved from one box to another. When she was through changing those things around, it was found that everything was in practically the same place as before.

Now she started running from this corner to that. Here she picked up something which she put down in another place, only to take it away from that place and carry it back to where it had first been. There was not much she could move around: one pot, several potsherds (all in use), a spoon, a rag, a bundle. For a while she stopped altogether. Holding one fist against her mouth, she stood thinking. Then she hurried to a corner. She bent down upon a wooden box made into a sort of trunk, which was the wardrobe of the family. She opened it and with both hands she rummaged around inside it, having obviously forgotten what she wanted. After much aimless digging into that box, picking things up and pushing them back again, she finally dragged out a bundle of marine-blue cotton goods, all crumpled and wrinkled and partly smutty and stained. Holding it up against the light, she turned it round and round without saying a word about what she meant to do with it.

All this time Manuel was sitting on an old sack half full of

124

corn-cobs. His chin resting on his breast, his hat covering all of his face, his dead kid brother lying in his outstretched arms, which were lying on his knees, he sat there motionless and serene as if he were a god made of bronze.

Sleigh appeared in the open entrance. On his head he carried a table, the only one he owned. He worked it through the narrow doorway and put it on the floor in the middle of the hut. Then the pump-master woman stepped forward and spread two bed-sheets over the crude table.

Manuel now rose, went to the table, laid the kid gently on it, and walked out into the night without once looking back.

The Garcia ran to the table, took the cold, wet, crumpled hands of her baby into her own, and pressed them together as though she wanted to fill them with new warmth. She noted that his head hung down on the table with the chin sticking up and she saw that blood was trickling out of his mouth and nose again, leaving little pink ribbons from the corners of his mouth down his chin and neck. It was strange that out of this body that had been dead so long, after having been in the water for more than four hours, there should still flow blood. But the blood was getting more and more watery.

It hurt the mother to see the little head in such an awkward position. She went to her bed, took a bunch of grass, and returned with it to the table. Half-way back she stopped, looked at her baby, and let the grass drop. A woman hurried out of the jacal and came back in a few seconds with a small soiled pillow.

The pump-master woman ransacked the Garcia's box, picked up a few green rags, sewed them together as a bag, stuffed grass from the bed into it and pushed it under the kid's head, so that instead of one he now had two pillows, and the head was now in the natural position of sleep.

On the two pillows and the bed-sheets watery pink blots soon appeared, which widened slowly into large stains.

The mother took off his shoes, which, I noticed, covered the

125

ankles and were therefore more like low boots than shoes. I understood better why that kid had felt helpless in such stiff, heavy shoes. The Garcia also took off his new socks, his short pants, and she pulled off his shirt, which was so small for him that it couldn't be buttoned anywhere.

The pump-master woman searched for a comb. At first she parted his hair at the left. She looked at her job, did not like it, and parted the hair at the right.

The roosters crowed for the second time during the night. It was one hour after midnight.

Picking up from the ground the piece of blue cotton goods which she had dropped some time before, the Garcia spread and flattened it, and it turned out to be a cheap little sailor suit. It was the kid's Sunday suit and he had been very proud of it, because not even the pump-master's boys had anything like it.

The mother now dressed her baby in that sailor suit.

When this was done I looked at the kid, and horror crept down my back. In his torn and patched-up pants and in his dirty shirt with half a hundred holes in it, and with that funny-looking bit of string across his shoulders, the kid was very pretty in his way. In fact he was a real and natural-looking child of the jungle. He belonged here. But in that cheap sailor suit he no longer looked like a son of his native land. Yet somehow the clean-cut, noble features of a full-blooded Indian finally triumphed over the pale-faced, flat-footed Syrian jobbers and peddlers who had to sell cheaper and cheaper still if they wanted to sell at all.

While alive the kid had worn that suit only once, at a feria more than a year ago.

Neither the coat nor the pants could now be buttoned. In the first place the kid had outgrown the suit; in the second place his body was swollen with water. His mother was trying again and again to get the suit properly fixed. In vain. After many fruitless attempts she suddenly got impatient and began

126

to twist and press the body until finally she was able to button the suit. The suit was now so tight that I expected it to burst any minute. She wrung out the wet socks and held them up to the little fire burning on the earthen floor. When the socks had dried she put them on his feet. Then she put on his new shoes.

During the time she was working on the kid she sniffed audibly and blew her nose every ten seconds or so into her fingers. Then she moaned and sighed deeply. Now and then she blubbered, but no one could understand what she said. Frequently she looked around the room, picked up a rag, and blew her nose into it. Her body trembled every once in a while with inner convulsions. But she uttered no more loud cries, perhaps because she forgot to do so in her concentration on her job of dressing the kid for his last trip.

The people inside the hut whispered, murmured. She paid no attention to anyone. It seemed that she thought herself entirely alone in the room. Whatever she did was done correctly. Nevertheless one got the impression that she was in a dream and that she acted automatically.

On one wall of the jacal there was a crude shelf. On it stood a little picture of the Holy Virgin of Guadalupe painted on glass. On either side of that cheap picture there were other, smaller pictures of saints. No image of the Lord could be seen anywhere. The pictures of the saints had short prayers printed on the back, which neither Garcia nor his wife could read. In front of the Holy Virgin there stood an ordinary drinking-glass, slightly cracked, which was filled with oil on which floated a tiny paraffin candle, no bigger than a match, stuck through a piece of tin the size of a dime. This tiny candle was lighted and it burned day and night to illuminate with its faint flame the picture of the Madre Santisima. The light was supposed to burn day and night, but often the Garcias did not have the few centavitos for oil because other things less eternal were needed more urgently. There was no oil in the glass when the pump-master woman had come to look after things. One of her first acts had been to fill the glass with fresh oil and light the candle. What would all these people have thought of the Garcia family if they had found the light for the Holy Virgin dead? They would have thought the house inhabited by pagans or, worse, by a godless gringo. The light was no more than just a glimmer, yet it satisfied the faithful and no devil could come in now to snatch a soul away.

The little shelf, at least to the Garcia family, was not only the house altar. It was at the same time the place for miscellaneous secular things needed in the house. On it were standing withered flowers in several broken pots. There, also, wrapped in a piece of newspaper, were what the Garcia called her sewing utensils—that is, a few rags, a few partly rusty needles, a few pins, and pieces of white and black thread wound around a strip of brown packing paper. There were also a comb, a dozen hairpins, matches, and Carlosito's toys, including a broken tin automobile worth a dime, a fish-hook, a sling made out of a piece of automobile tube, a broken cork, a small, brightly colored glass ball used as a marble, two brass buttons, a few colored pictures of the kind one finds in cigarette packages. And there was the little ukulele, his treasured gift from Manuel, with which he had wanted to form a dance orchestra with his fiddle-playing father. From one corner of the shelf a cheap rosary dangled. In a little cup which once had belonged to a doll's kitchen, a few centavos were piled, and a few more bronze coins were lying near it. The total could not have been more than thirty-five centavos, the whole fortune of the house.

From a thin wire tied to a pole in the roof, a reed basket was hanging. It contained the family's few provisions, two little cones of unrefined brown sugar, a few ounces of ground coffee wrapped in greasy paper, a pound of rice of the cheapest kind, a few pounds of black beans, and half a dozen green and red chile husks. Two bottles were tied to the basket. In one of them there was salt—crude, large grains which looked old and dirty. One third of the other bottle was filled with lard, which in this region never hardens and must therefore be kept in bottles. If it were kept in an open vessel it would be found full of drowned ants. As in all the other homes, this basket was hung up to protect its contents from rats and mice. But the rats in this region were such excellent acrobats that they climbed down from the grass roof along the thin wire without difficulty, and, of course, stole the provisions; for the Lord in His infinite wisdom has so made the world that no one is so poor that he cannot be robbed by another, and no one is so strong that he cannot be killed by somebody else.

On the earthen floor near the wall a fire was smoldering. It was the family hearth. An earthen pot filled with coffee stood close to the fire. Obviously it had been left there early in the evening so that Garcia would be able to gulp hot coffee in the morning when returning from the dance. Next to the fire, leaning against the wall, there was the usual piece of sheet iron on which to heat tortillas. Then there were three earthen pots, two earthen vessels, none of them whole, an old, rusty iron pan, and the metate, the big concave stone in which boiled corn is ground for the dough out of which tortillas are made.

The choza had a second, very small room. It was formed by a wall made of sticks tied together with lianas. This wall was about six feet high and ran parallel to the outer wall, forming a separate compartment five feet wide and three-fourths of the hut in length. That narrow side room was filled with old sacks, a shabby Mexican saddle, two home-made, wooden pack saddles of the most primitive kind, many old ropes and lassos, an old basket for the hens to lay their eggs in. The few chickens the Garcias had roosted in a near-by tree, as no other shelter was provided for them. From a spike in this compartment the Garcia's week-day dress was hanging. It was very ragged and very dirty.

On the floor of this narrow side room there was a bast mat on which lay a fairly good blanket. This was the bed in which Manuel slept while he was here. In the camp in the Texas oil fields where he worked he was provided with a decent cot, two clean sheets, and two clean army blankets, but, like all his fellow workers, he would grumble daily about the stinginess of the rich oil companies. Of course, there he worked and helped the company make millions of dollars, while here he was on vacation having a good time. And that made all the difference, which lots of people can't grasp.

23

 More candles were brought in by friendly neighbors. They were lighted and two were set near the boy's head and two near his feet. Two had been set in front of the picture of the Madre Santisima. Because of these candles, and because so many people were coming in and going out and moving around inside the house, and especially because the women were dressed in their best, the jacal had lost its poor appearance. It looked almost like a little country chapel on Christmas Eve.

The majority of the people stayed outside. Anyway, there would not have been room enough in the choza for the hundred or more persons who were now here. They squatted on the ground outside the hut, where they smoked and chatted in low voices. Now and then a few women or men entered the hut, while others left to make room for the newcomers.

Manuel's younger brother, the one who was considered half-witted, squatted on the ground, right by the entrance, where he was weeping quietly. No one paid any attention to him. Nor did he pay any to the people passing by, although occasionally they pushed him unintentionally. It was not clear whether he wept for his little stepbrother or because he saw the women weeping or because for the moment he did not know what else he could do. No one asked him anything and no one consoled him. He was the only stranger present, now that I had been accepted by the crowd as a fellow mourner.

Manuel entered as though he were sneaking in. He looked at the kid, went to the shelf, took the tin comb, and parted the kid's hair at the other side. For this simple job he took a long time.

The pump-master woman, standing between the body and the shelf, was working with strips of gold, silver, red, blue, and green paper, which she had produced from the devil knows where, to make a little crown which would be set on the kid's head. When that crown was ready a little cross was fastened to the top. A man had cut this cross out of an old tin can with his pocket knife while the pump-master woman was making the crown. With a few drops of hot paraffin from a candle the cross was covered with gold paper. Repeatedly the woman measured the kid's skull with a thread to make sure the crown would fit. Her tears rolled down her cheeks and dropped on the colored paper, and every once in a while she had to dry her tears because she couldn't see through them. Whenever she put the little crown on the kid's head to see whether it fitted, the crown looked more beautiful than before, and she smiled under her tears. And each time she took it off she had a new idea how to make it still more beautiful.

The two men who were busy stretching the kid's legs finally shaped them to everybody's satisfaction. A board on which rested a heavy stone was laid across the knees to prevent them from returning to their unnatural position.

I noted that his mouth was wide open. It did not disturb me a bit. Why, I thought it only natural for a little boy who looks suddenly at another and entirely different world to open his mouth wide for sheer astonishment. No one he would meet on his trip would take offense on account of it. His mother, however, thought differently. She wanted to have a beautiful dead baby. She tried to close that little mouth, but it would not stay closed. I asked for a strip of an old shirt. Having obtained it, I tied it round his face so that the lower jaw was kept firmly pressed against the upper, and I made a sort of tie under his chin, so that the meaning of the strip was concealed.

If any of the neighbors or visitors got busy on the kid nobody paid much attention. But as soon as I went near the body and touched it, all the people came around and many from the outside hurried in. It seemed they thought that I might still be able to perform a great miracle, even bring the kid back to life. A foreigner is always, everywhere, believed to be gifted with strange powers. That I might do any harm to the kid, even now after his death, no longer occurred to them. I had known them only three days, but I learned a few days later that they had known me for a long time. My fame rested on a story told about me far and wide which also had to do with a dead Indian; it was said that after he had been dead for seven hours he was brought back to life by me, or, to tell the truth, was nearly brought back to life by me. At least I had made him breathe once more and, in the opinion of all the Indians concerned, I would have raised him from the dead had it not been for a gachupin, a most hated Spaniard, who entered the scene at the crucial moment and ordered a treatment contrary to the one I had applied. Everybody in the Indian village where that had happened was convinced that I could raise Indians from the dead if I was left to do it my own way.

The dressing of the kid's jaw was approved by everybody in the hut and I was raised in the estimation of the mourning community.

With the help of a man, the pump-master woman now folded the kid's arms across his chest and tried to put the hands

133

in the position they would take in prayer. Neither the arms nor the hands obeyed. Apparently the pump-master woman had learned from what she thought was my invention, for she and her helper tied strings around the little arms and hands. The strings cut deep into the swollen, spongy flesh.

The kid had the crown on his head by now. It was really astonishing how the pump-master woman had been able to make a very becoming piece of headwear, a little work of art, out of such primitive material. If one did not look closely, one would not believe that the crown had been made of paper. Were it not for that horrible sailor suit, a suit which made one laugh and weep at the same time, the child would not look like a little boy who had been born and brought up in a poor Indian choza, but more like the son of a dethroned Aztec king of old whose high rank and dignity had been restored after his death.

The pump-master woman contemplated the body for a while with a smile on her lips. A new idea entered her mind. She found him not quite beautiful enough for her taste and her neighborly love. She left the hut and then returned with a thin stick, around which she wound gold paper. When everything was done, a golden scepter had been made, with a little golden cross at the top. This she put in the kid's right hand after loosening the strings.

Just as she finished this job, old man Garcia returned from his trip to Tlalcozautitlan and entered the choza. For a long while he remained standing at the door. Then, without showing by any gesture what was going on in his mind, he looked at his little prince. He took off his hat and stepped up to the table.

The kid was to him not just a boy; he was not just the youngest and therefore the most petted and the most beloved. This little boy meant far more to him than his other two. Having had the luck to be loved by a pretty woman who was

134

half his age, he had seen in that child the assurance of a happy life with his young wife, permanent proof to her and to all the other men that she had made no mistake when she had married him.

All the people present in the hut stared at him to see how he would take it. Everybody knew how much he loved that kid of his, the only one he had had by his young wife and most likely the last he could expect.

He looked at the body with empty eyes as if there were nothing before him. He did not understand it, could not grasp the cold fact that the kid was dead and that he would never again hear him bustle about the house and climb up his back and ride on his neck when he returned from work in the bush. He turned around and gazed at the floor as if he were looking for something. When he raised his head again, thick tears like little crystal balls were running down his cheeks. He did not ask when, where, or how. He stood for a minute near the door, his head leaning wearily against the door post, then left the hut.

A few men, his intimate friends, went after him. He did not see them. He left the yard, mounted the horse on which he had come, and rode out into the darkness.

24

 As there was nothing I could do inside at the moment, I too left the hut. Outside, in the yard, men, women, and children were lying all about, huddled up and asleep. Others squatted on the ground talking. Others were walking around. Out of every choza in the settlement dim lights were shining.

Burros brayed plaintively in the prairie. The jungle was singing its eternal song of joy, love, sadness, pain, tragedy, hope, despair, victory, defeat. What did the jungle or the bush care about the things which had happened here? To the jungle, men are of no account. It does not even accept men's dung, leaving it to flies and beetles. But it does take men's bones after the buzzards, ants, and maggots have been satisfied. What is man to the jungle? He takes a few trees out, or a few shrubs, or he clears a patch to build a jacal and plant some corn and beans or a few coffee trees. If man forgets that patch for but three months, it is no longer his; the jungle has taken it back. Man comes, man goes, the jungle stays on. If man does not fight it daily, it devours him.

I walked over to Sleigh, whose hut was only about thirty yards away. He was blowing on the fire and his face was red. The coffee seemed to be ready. It was not good coffee. It was stale, ground weeks, if not months, ago.

"Won't you have a cup?" Sleigh asked the moment he saw me.

"You'd better take some over to the women first, mister, they need it badly, they're breaking down."

"Okay, if you say so. It's your loss. Never mind, I'll cook another pot and you can have as much as you like of that. The woman left two pounds with me. Anyway, I think we need some hot coffee just as badly as others do."

The girl lying on her petate spread out on the ground and hidden under her mosquito bar, slept soundly. Perhaps Sleigh had told her about the kid. She did not care. He was not hers. She had hers in her arms—and what else was there to worry about? She made no pretense that she might also belong to that great world community of mothers. She was on her own.

"Get those cups, please, and help me carry them over to the women." Sleigh winked at a box on which were standing seven enameled cups of different sizes, four of them battered so badly that no enamel was left. Two were leaking, Sleigh explained, and he said the people who used them would have to gulp like hell if they wanted to get some coffee.

"By all means leave two here for us. I don't like to drink coffee out of my hat if I can help it. Let's hoof."

I took the cups and we returned to the Garcia's. Sleigh put the cups and the pot on the floor, poured coffee, and offered the Garcia woman the first cup. Automatically she drank the hot coffee with one gulp. The pump-master woman and a few others took some sips. None drank the whole cupful, but only part of it, handing the rest to the woman next to her.

The pump-master woman rolled a cigarette. Then she handed the little bag with black tobacco to the Garcia, who also started smoking after rolling her own. She did not sit down, but kept hustling without doing anything definite. The truth was that there was nothing anybody could do now.

After the women had sat around for some time smoking cigarettes or cigars and sipping hot coffee, they felt that they had to get busy. Using old shirts and dresses and bright-colored rags, they designed coverlets and fancy ribbons to adorn the kid and the coffin in which he was to be laid.

Sleigh winked at me, seeming to feel out of place now, as I did too. So we went back to his hut.

There we sat near the smoking little tin bottle which was his lamp. I blinked at the fire on the hearth, on which had been set an old enameled pot full of water to make fresh coffee.

"Listen, Sleigh, where do you get the water you consume in your household?"

He eyed me as if he had not heard me well.

"Yes, I mean the water you have in that bucket."

"Well, my eyes, such a question! That water? I guess it's big enough for you to see where the water came from."

"You don't mean to tell me that you get the water out of that river?" I repeated the question, spoke very clearly, because I saw him staring at me as if he doubted my sanity.

"And what do you think? You don't expect me or anybody here to order water in sealed beer-bottles from Kansas City or by air mail from Yosemite Valley, do you? You shouldn't ask such a dumb question because I always believed you were a guy with some brains—sometimes, I mean, not always. Don't misunderstand me. Look here, wise guy, when I met you the first time down at that stinking pool in the jungle where I had to stick you up to save my skin from a jungle-mad greeny, didn't I see you lap up that stinking water as if it were ice-cold beer, or did I? That time you didn't ask who had spit in it or what mule had let go into it only half an hour before. You drank it all right, and you were pretty happy to have found that muddy hole with some water still in it!"

138

"All right, all right, you win. But now how about the water for our coffee out of that river?"

He grinned at me. "All the water you have drunk since you came here was from the river. You don't expect me to boil the water first or, as you would call it, deseenfaict it before we drink it? Don't make me laugh."

"You know pretty well what I'm talking about. I'm not referring to the water I drank yesterday or today. I'm talking of the water in which only a few hours ago and only a hundred or a hundred and fifty yards from here that kid was drowned."

"And what of it? Was that kid poison or what? His mother drank the coffee we brought, didn't she? And she liked the coffee, didn't she? Well, she didn't ask me that damn foolish question of yours—where I got the water for the coffee she drank! She knew what water that coffee was made of, and if she, the mother, can drink the coffee, you aren't too good to criticize it. We're thankful to the Lord for giving it to us and that we have water all the year round, while there are hundreds of thousands of families in this republic who have no water for months and have to leave their homes and fields in search of it, taking along all their chickens and goats and what have you."

Sleigh was right. He might not be interested in reading a full column in a newspaper at one sitting, but he was right. I should not have thought of that little spongy body and of the blood dripping out of his mouth, his nose, and his skull.

After a long silence Sleigh said: "God, I say all this doesn't interest me a damn bit. Water is water, and as long as I can drink it without getting cramps in my belly, I consider it good water and I thank God for it, if He wants me to, even on my knees. No, it isn't that. What interests me about that water is quite another thing. What I mean is that board with the candle on it. That's what got me shivering all over. I'm still not feeling very comfortable along my spine, frankly speaking. It's a remarkable thing, that board and the candle on it. My woman has told me about it before. They also do it where she comes from. She belongs to another region and another sort of people or what you may call another tribe. But they do it just like here. And I tell you, man, that candle always finds the drowned."

"Always?"

"Always, that's what I say. My wife has told me that the board can even sail upstream against a very strong current if the drowned man lies in that direction."

"I doubt that and nobody can make me believe it." I meant it. "No Indian can do anything more than we can do, and no Indian knows more than we. No colored man, no man of any other race, no Chinese, no Hindu, no Tibetan can perform miracles we cannot perform. That's all nonsense. We think other races mysterious only because we don't understand their language well enough and we don't understand their customs and their ways of living and doing things. It's because of this lack of understanding them that we believe them capable of performing all sorts of miracles and mysterious acts. I personally have found out that on a long march through the jungle or the bush I can stand thirst and hunger just as easy as my Indian boys, and many times even better."

"That may be so. Anyway, it has little if anything to do with what I'm talking about," Sleigh said. "I've got my experiences too, and as far as I know, you are right in what you speak about. We've got more energy, or, better, more strong will—still better, we've got a better-trained will than the primitive. These people don't think it worth while to have a strong will. They ask why have it if it's only a nuisance and extra work. It's only we, who want to exploit them, who wish to train their wills and energies so that we can enslave them easier and get better workers and force them into the trap of installment slavery so that they are never free and have to do our bidding because we've got the better-trained will and energy. But to come back to the point, you'll admit that there are Indians who let themselves be bitten by a rattler half a dozen times, or let themselves be stung by scorpions or what have you, and it doesn't do them any harm. On the other hand if a rattler bites you or the red scorpion gets you, there is a dead guy in less than twenty hours."

"Not every one of them is immune against such poisons. I've seen Indians die of snake-bites as quickly and surely as any white man."

"Right. That's because not every one of them knows the proper medicine."

"Exactly. That's just it. If we knew the proper medicine we would be as immune as some of them are or pretend to be. And you know that they die from calenture and other fevers and diseases in most cases quicker than a white man who just takes ordinary care of himself."

Sleigh nodded pensively. "Why not, I ask. Why not? They're humans, or ain't they? So they have to die somehow or other." He stood up, went to the fire, stirred it up, blew at it, and pushed the pot closer to the flames.

Having sat down again, he said: "All right, all right, if you wish to insist that no mysterious and hidden powers have worked in this particular case—I mean powers and mysteries which only the natives know about and can command—then perhaps you can explain why that board sailed to the kid and actually found him where no man had looked."

"I admit I don't know. Not yet. Perhaps I can find an explanation some time later. I have to think it over. I only deny any mystery whatever behind it. It is absolutely natural, the whole thing. So far I don't even know in which direction to go to find out the truth."

While vaguely thinking about where I could find an explanation of how the board was made to sail towards the body, there came to my mind another method by which a drowned man could be found, which I remembered having seen once back home in the States.

So I said: "Look here, Sleigh, I'll tell you that we are not so much dumber than the Indians. I remember a time, when I was a boy, that a drowned man was found in a way which at first looked very mysterious to me. Later, however, when I had time to think it over, I found the explanation. It seems a man had drowned in a lake when fishing. His canoe had turned over. The lake was searched for two days and the body could not be found. So on the third day cans filled with dynamite were let down in the lake and blown up. The body soon came to the surface. I still remember that everybody talked of supernatural powers which had been at work to give the body back to his family for a Christian burial. The minister didn't overlook the chance to mention it in church, telling the congregation that the finding of the body was the visible result of the ardent prayers of the bereaved family and that the mighty and merciful hand of the Lord could easily be seen in that mysterious occurrence. The people explained it in a different way. They said that the lake likes to be quiet and calm, so when it is stirred up violently, it will immediately spit out the body to get back to its quiet condition. When I became older I learned the truth. Any drowned human or animal body, even a dead fish if it is big enough, will and must come to the surface sooner or later, sometimes inside of twenty-four hours, though sometimes it may take three days. But if that body is held down by water plants or shrubs or by heavy clothing, or if it is stuck in the mud, it cannot come up. In that case if the bottom of the lake is stirred up by a bomb, the body is freed and comes up."

"Well," Sleigh said, "there is no mystery about that. Anyone can see that. I could have told you so before you explained it. Dynamite will blow up anything under heaven, even huge

142

mountains and rock, so why not a human body? Don't tell me bedtime stories. In this case here, man, it won't be so easy for you to explain why that board sailed to the kid as if a captain were sitting on it. And you may believe me, Gales, I've lived long enough among these natives—now a generation, I would say—and I've seen things, my God, remarkable things and strange things which no professor of any American or even Bolshevik college could ever explain, no matter how smart and learned he may say he is. I won't tell you all the things I've seen here. It would be a waste of time, since you wouldn't believe any of them, as I know you don't believe in anything. You are one of the wise guys. Why, I'm sure you don't even believe in ghosts. I do and I could tell you lots about them. But what's the use with a guy like you? The mother of my woman can speak with her dead relatives. What do you say now?—It's no use. Forget it. Want another cup of coffee? Help yourself. There's plenty of it."

He was right, Sleigh was. It was no use discussing such things with him. He had been living too long with these people and so he had accepted all their beliefs. He believed anything strange he saw or heard of, the same way the Indians did. He wanted to believe them and he never tried to find any sort of natural explanation. That was why such arguments with him moved in a circle and never got beyond. The fact is I was not interested in explaining what I had seen that night. All the events were clear to me. No mystery of any sort. I was under no spell and there was no auto-suggestion. I was not even sleepy or tired. I was fully awake and my mind was fresh. Of course I had no witness. Sleigh was no witness. His criticisms, as far as he criticized anything at all, did not count when dealing with affairs in which Indians were the actors. He thought all Indians possessed mysterious powers and great knowledge of the supernatural. He believed everything they told him or that he heard from his wife. He might doubt the virginity of the Lord's mother, but he never doubted the beliefs of the Indians.

Perhaps it was the environment. Perhaps it was his unshakable faith. I was surprised to find myself beginning to dodge an explanation and I felt a certain comfort in not trying to think things through to the end. And why should I not have let the whole matter rest? One lives easier, happier, more in harmony with the universe, if one does not work one's brain continually about things of which the explanations and analyses cannot make us any happier, usually not even richer, if it is riches we are after. Take life as it is. Here in the jungle, perhaps all over the world, that is the whole meaning of life. What else do you want? What else do you expect? Anything else is negation of life and it is nonsense besides. It is the nonsense out of which grow every heartache, every grief, every evil in the world.

25

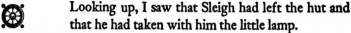 Looking up, I saw that Sleigh had left the hut and that he had taken with him the little lamp.

In front of me, on the creaking wicker chair that was so old and shaky that it was sheer wonder how anybody could sit on it without breaking through, sat Perez, the Indian who had fished the kid out of the water. How he had come to be sitting there so suddenly, so unexpectedly, I did not know. I must have been dreaming or asleep while trying to make the world a better place to live in happily. My first impression was that by some magic Sleigh had been changed into Perez.

"Listen, Perez, you promised me two yellowhoods, two young ones, this morning. When do I get them?"

"I haven't been in the bush for some time. I won't go next week either. No time, you know, mister." He was sitting with his legs spread wide apart and his hands dangling down between them.

"Why don't you go in the bush, Señor Perez? Don't you burn charcoal any more?"

"Well, now see here, mister, it's this way. The gringo that is

145

living up there on the hill where the best trees for charcoal are to be had and where I know the finest yellowhoods you've ever seen in all your life are nesting, well, that goddamned gringo, may he go straight to hell, well, he says, that liar says, that I've stolen one of his mules. That's a lie. It's the biggest lie I've ever heard in all my life. And he says that I'm a damned bandit and a bandolero and a cabrón too and that my poor mother is a damned bitch, that's what he says, and he calls himself an educated gringo that has gone to school. But the worst of it, I tell you, mister, is that I, poor Indian as I am, I can do nothing against him, absolutely nothing. I have to suffer it. So you see here, señor, there is no chance to get you the two yellowhoods I promised you, which would learn to speak in no time. That's why I told you that redhoods are no good. It must be yellowhoods. But it's a big damned lie. I am no bandit. I can swear it."

"I don't think you're a bandit, Señor Perez, and I don't believe that you ever stole a mule."

"That's the naked truth, mister. And I can see that you are an educated caballero. I can swear by the Most Holy Virgin in heaven and by the Holy Child also that I know nothing of a stolen mule. If I were a bandit, I tell you, I'd go to hell myself and of my own free will. That gringo up there, he isn't honest. He says he has seen the tracks of my feet right beside those of his mule, which he can recognize, so he says, by the iron shoes, and he says he has seen my tracks and those of his mule right together outside the fence of his pasture and he says he has followed these tracks—I don't know where to, because he doesn't say. Never in all my life did I ever go where he says he has seen my huaraches beside the irons of his mule. How do I know who has stolen his mule? It's none of my business."

"Well, Perez, I've been told that Mister Erskin has said the mule he lost is worth around two hundred and fifty pesos."

"Bueno, señor, right there you can see what sort of liar that gringo is. Do you know what I've been offered for that mule? Forty pesos I've been offered, and not a single red centavito more have I been paid for that mule by those miserable robbers down there in Llerra. This I swear is the truth. And then this gringo tells the world the mule is worth two hundred and fifty pesos in cold cash and en efectivo. That's the kind of gringos we have around here, who we have to suffer humiliation from. I can only laugh, that's the only thing I can do. And now, to make things still worse, that Americano comes along and says I've stolen his mule. You must admit that's no way to treat poor inoffensive people like us, and in our own country too. But what can we do? Nothing. Just suffer. That's what we can do."

While he was sitting before me and talking, I could barely see him, because all the light we now had in the hut was the fire on the hearth. And that was not much.

Perez rose, went to the fire, and lit the cigarette he had been rolling while telling me the story of the stolen mule.

Sleigh returned with the little tin bottle lamp and an earthen pot filled with fresh milk.

"The cow has come home at last," he said on entering. "The damned devil may know where that poor animal has been all night."

From a soiled paper bag he dug out coffee with his bare hand, which was dirty from handling the cows. Two handfuls of coffee he threw into the boiling water. The coffee foamed and ran over into the fire, which sizzled angrily. He took hold of the pot with a rag and set it down on the floor beside us.

"You'll get my cup in a minute," he said to Perez.

"That's all right by me, don't bother," the Indian answered.

"Listen, Perez, was that kid lying flat on the bottom or what was his position?" Sleigh asked.

"No, he wasn't exactly at the bottom. He didn't even touch the bottom so far as I could make out. His feet and hands were stuck in water shrubs. He was, in a way, sitting in the shrubs. If you ask me, I don't believe he would ever have come up if we hadn't dragged him out. The plants held him like the many arms of an ugly monster."

"How did you know, Perez, that the kid was stuck just at that place and in no other?" I asked.

"That was very easy to know," he said. "There was no mystery about that. The light was standing right above him. You could see that for yourself. Anyone could have fished him out after the light had settled over him."

"Yes, I saw the light standing there above him. Only the question is, how did the light know he was there?"

"Nothing simpler than that, mister. The kid was calling the light to come to him and show us the way. So the light had to obey, and it came. There is nothing strange about that. It's quite natural. Anyone can see that."

Sleigh laughed right out. "Well, there you heard it with your own ears. Are you satisfied now?" He grinned at me. "Any more foolish questions now? I told you so before. It's all quite natural. Nothing strange about it. That's the whole mystery. In fact, there is no mystery at all. Here the Indians can't practice any more magic than you can or me. The kid calls the light and the light has to obey orders and goes to him. Everything is as clear and bright as sunlight. That's all natural. That's what I told you all the time."

No use. So I spoke again to the man who seemed still to be the saner of the two. "Well, Perez, now what about the two young yellowhoods?"

"I don't go up in the bush. Besides there would be no reason for going there now. They started to sit only a few days ago. I know it. A friend who had been up there told me. Why should I crawl through that damn thorny thicket if I can't get any. Because there are none to be had just at this time of the

148

year. Two months later it will be easy and you can have a half-dozen if you wish."

He had his coffee now and was sipping it slowly like a critical connoisseur of drinks. Sleigh poured me another cup and took the rest of the pot over to the Garcia's party.

After a short while he returned, went to the hearth, and lit a new cigarette. Then he squatted Indian fashion on the floor facing Perez and me, who were sitting on his rotten wicker chairs.

The baby of the girl under the mosquito bar whined softly. From the movement of the bar and by the gleam of the fire I saw the girl giving her baby to drink. Before the baby was satisfied, while he was still suckling, the girl snored again so heavily that the hut trembled.

Both Perez and Sleigh got sleepy, let their heads drop upon their chests, and blinked into emptiness. In his sleep Sleigh sensed that his cigarette had gone out. He rose swaying as if he were drunk and walked in a shuffling manner to the hearth. His cigarette again lit, he leaned against a post and dozed off again.

He slept only a few minutes. He woke up and walked to the door. Looking up to the sky, which had begun to clear and in which a few stars could be seen now, he said: "It is just past two. I thought it later."

I looked at my watch and said: "Twenty past."

"I'll have to go to milk the cows now or they'll get restless and start for the prairie. Perez, are you coming with me?"

"Of course, vamonos!" He was so fast asleep that his cigarette had dropped without his being aware of it. Now he looked for it, lit it, and followed Sleigh, who, with a bucket in one hand, had already walked off to the corral.

He shouted back: "Hey, Gales, why don't you turn in for a coupla hours? You must be dog-tired and it will surely do you lots of good. Don't you bother about me, man, I've got to get

149

busy with them cows, you know. Hi, Perez, where are you? Are you coming?"

Perez, just leaving the hut, said: "Now, don't you holler, amigo. Here I am, always on the spot, just call on me for any trouble. Who, por la Santisima, put that damned log right in my way? Anyone could break his neck here, what with all sorts of sticks, logs, and stones lying about."

26

  As Perez had taken the little lamp with him, the hut was dark once more. A few forlorn embers gleamed on the hearth.

I was left alone and since I did not know what better I could do, I groped my way towards the corner where the bed I had slept in last night and the night before was. It wasn't a bed in the true sense of the word. It was more like a corrupted hammock.

The bed in which Sleigh and his wife slept was shoved against one wall. It was similar to the one the Garcias had, but the network was made more carefully and the mattress consisted of a softer fiber. The corner in which the family bed stood was separated from the main room by a wall of sticks six feet high. The sticks which formed that wall were so far apart that one could put his finger between them. To get some privacy Sleigh's woman had put up on this wall a few pieces of threadbare cotton goods.

Well, I was tired. I took off my boots, unfastened my belt, and, sailor fashion, crawled into that hammock, which only the greedy landlady of a cheap boardinghouse would call a cot.

Bridges, rivers without a downstream current, mule-drivers yelling for more coffee, alligators, asthmatic pumps which cough, queens of England waving a ragged handkerchief, bodies of little babies, naked Indians (some of them armless), black-haired heads popping out of prairie grass, lighted candles swimming under water like fish, cows with cougars on their necks, mouth-organs which play by themselves nailed to bridge posts, bandits riding on white burros, a picture of the Holy Virgin singing on a fiddle, Canada vanished from the earth and leaving mere emptiness behind, a few blurred lines from a Kansas City paper printed in Texas on a goat ranch, an oil well cemented with a splash in the water caused by a jumping bean, a girl with flowers in her hair dancing with a steel spring mattress which belongs to the president, a young woman with wreaths of fire-red flowers wound around her knees bent in an awkward position and crying: "No, no, I won't, I won't, don't you dare, no, no, I say no and no," battered enameled cups without bottoms but full of hot coffee and flying across a white table on which a sailor suit is weeping bitterly, a five-gallon hat walking through the night with no face under it—no, to hell with it, I could not sleep. Maybe it was the coffee. My head whirled. Yet I was as tired as a coal-heaver on a death ship. At last I dozed off, but not for long and I saw Mr. Erskin lying at the bottom of the river moving his hands and shouting: "Bring me a lantern which will obey orders, a lantern, please, a lantern for all my mules!" The water was very deep, twenty feet past two in the morning, but still I could see him because the water was lighted at the bottom. I didn't know Mr. Erskin, I had never seen him, yet I knew it was he who sat on eggs and hatched grown-up yellowhoods which sang a song about oilmen who made cigars out of cement. Nobody but me could see Mr. Erskin lying in

152

the water and I shouted to the people: "There are two little American boots in the river." Nobody listened and they said: "We'd better put a crown on his head and say it is a scepter of the Toltecs." Chinamen were coming and there was an explosion in the lake and a coffee pot drowned in a sack half filled with corn-cobs and held fast by alligators jumped high up in the air and a man dropped out of the pitch-dark clouds. He was an aviator milking a cow which had come home late and drunk, telling a little tin bottle lamp that two tigers and two lions went to a dance with the musicians stuck deep in the mud. And again dynamite was thrown in the lake and it exploded with a hundred reverberations.

It was this explosion of dynamite that awoke me. There was another explosion, and still another and another. I was fully awake now and I heard shots being fired outside the hut.

I got up and put my boots on. There was no longer any hope of getting some sleep.

It was still night. Peeping through the wall, I saw the little flame of the tin lamp by the corral where Sleigh was milking the cows and Perez, holding the lamp, squatted beside him. I could hear their voices, although I could not understand what they were talking about.

Boots on and belt fastened, I went to the door.

At the Garcia's yard there was a huge bonfire throwing its flames high up into the air. By this light I saw a score of Indians dismounting from their horses and firing their guns at the dark sky.

I went closer to see what was up.

The news of the kid's disappearance had already traveled more than ten miles in every direction, in spite of the night, in spite of the fact that the nearest telephone was a hundred miles from here. Although old man Garcia was one of the poorest Indians of the region, he was beloved by all, for some reason or other. Therefore as soon as the people had heard the news, they had left their beds and homes and come to offer their help. So far they knew only that the boy was missing. Nevertheless they had all brought fireworks to be used in the event that the kid should be found dead.

Among these Indians it is customary to ignite heaps of fireworks if a child dies, so that the angels in heaven will take notice that a new angelito is on his way up. Fireworks burnt at the death of an adult had the opposite consequences; that is to say, on hearing the fireworks the devil would wait close by the gate and look the newcomer over to see whether he might not be on his list. If it is a child, the angels, aroused by the fireworks, meet him half-way; and it does not matter whether the devil is at the gate, because he can do nothing with a child; an innocent child is not allowed to be registered on the devil's list, for he is still without sin.

The fireworks which had been brought were received and taken care of by the second brother, the half-wit. From this moment on he no longer had any interest in anything but the fireworks. He had long ago ceased to weep. For him the more joyful part of the funeral had now come.

The newly arrived had already heard that the kid had been found. One after another, with their hats off, they entered the hut to look at the kid and say a few consoling words to his mother. While in fact not much interested in how it happened, every one of them asked the mother to tell the story. Not from curiosity. Very wise men, they merely asked the mother in order to get her mind off the body.

Once she had started, the Garcia liked to tell the story from the very beginning. She told it over and over again, and always with the same words and with the same tone of voice and with the same emotions displayed at the same episode. By being repeated so often, it became more and more an ordinary story of everyday life. Even the emotions at the various points in her tale got to be almost like those of a bad actress, the oftener she

154

recited the narrative. She herself began to feel a certain distance from the event. She reached a point where she could tell it like a story she had heard from somebody else. It became impersonal to her. Her emotions were getting dull and leaving her heart and soul clearer every minute. Finally, when she was telling it for the twentieth time, she heard her own words sound like mere gossip.

She was beginning to take leave of her baby, without realizing it, at this moment.

She looked at him. To her astonishment she imagined that the boy lying dead on the table was not her baby any more. Her Carlosito was an active, lively little boy, forever talking and shouting and full of all sorts of mischief, who had to be spanked twice every day to keep him sensible and save him from himself. He was restless from the minute he opened his eyes in the morning until he closed them at night. That lump of ugly, clammy flesh with the smashed-in jaw and its arms held stiff across its chest, that could not be her baby. That had to be somebody else's baby, perhaps the baby she was just talking about. Hers wasn't so ugly. Everyone had told her how beautiful her Carlos was, one of the finest-looking kids for twenty miles around. The sailor suit, the crown, the scepter had made him a stranger to her. God knows where that child had come from. "What is he doing in my house, anyway?" she asked herself.

She wept now. And while she wept she realized, in sudden bewilderment, that she no longer wept only about her baby. She was now weeping about herself more than about the kid. She believed herself badly treated by fate, and unconsciously she began to hate many of the women present simply because they had babies at their breasts. She lamented the sad fact that she no longer had a child on whom she could heap her motherly love.

All these thoughts were running wild in her mind while her

mouth was telling the story that was stale from so much repeating. But through her thinking and brooding and analyzing in her primitive manner her thoughts, emotions, pains, and heartaches, she came to realize that she was not at all an exception. She looked around and noted the presence of seven other women who she knew had also lost children as dear to them as her baby had been to her. So she became conscious of the fact that she was but an average mother and not a mother selected by fate to suffer something extraordinary. What she suffered tonight, thousands, millions of mothers had suffered before her, a thousand were suffering the same in this very hour, and thousands of millions of mothers would suffer when she herself would again be happy.

Perhaps it was because she was so very tired, so exhausted, from worry, pain, and weeping and yelling, that she began to be herself once more.

27

 The Garcia's front yard was a sandy square open on two sides, while the other two were fenced in by thorny bushes. The hut was framed by a row of old rusty kerosene cans and broken vessels filled with earth in which flowers had been planted, some of which were now in full bloom. That conglomeration of old cans and potsherds with flowers in them was considered the Garcia's garden. Close to the hut on one side there was a wild chile shrub which daily provided the family with green pepper. Because there were so many visitors present, the bushes, thorny shrubs, and magueys were decorated with hats, diapers, shirts, rags, and blankets.

The whole place looked like a camp. Men, women, and children were sleeping on the ground or just dozing. Some were lying on mats, others on blankets, but most of them on the bare ground. Some people had put up mosquito bars, which looked like little tents. Bits of music played on mouth-organs fluttered about. The place was lighted by torches and campfires. There were also a few small lanterns and half a dozen of the usual open tin lamps.

157

Many boys were helping the half-witted son shoot off the firecrackers. No one was allowed to shoot them off but himself. The others were only permitted to stir up the fire and try out the firecrackers which had failed to go off the first time. The stepson's great day had come at last. He felt like a dictator among the boys who had to humiliate themselves before him to get the privilege of firing one occasionally. Two days later he would get his reward by being beaten up by all those whom he now refused a share in the game.

Many of the visitors had brought bottles of mescal, that very hard brandy distilled of mescal juice and tasting like rubbing alcohol blended with unrefined kerosene. Sometimes this brandy travels under the name of tequila; at other times it is called aguardiente, then again comiteco, also cuervo, or viuda, in some parts herradura, but whatever its name, it is always the same stuff.

The bottle went from mouth to mouth. One man, obviously with a heart of gold, took a bottle, entered the hut, removed his hat, and offered it to the Garcia woman. She looked at it, but she did not hesitate long. She took a shot of it that was equal to no less than three fingers of a hard-working peasant. Any sane white man who would whip into his belly a portion like the one the Garcia lashed down her throat, would be floored as if he'd been clubbed.

Among the Indians who arrived at this moment there was a very poor peasant. He was practically in rags, but they were clean. His horse had no saddle but a bast mat. He entered the hut with the others. He ran his eyes over the kid, then went up to the mother and told her how beautiful the kid was and how prettily dressed, like the Holy Child of the Madre Santisima in church, and that he was positive that the kid was already with the angels, so sweet did he look. The Garcia smiled proudly, straightened her whole body, and thanked him and the other men for their admiration and praise.

158

When that poor peasant came out of the hut, he looked around and found a bench that was not occupied at the moment. He sat down and drew out an old book which looked like a prayer book. For a few minutes he leafed through it as if to find the right page. Then he began to sing.

Unable to read, he knew by heart all the words he sang. He looked into the book only because he had seen people in church looking into such a book when they sang.

Most stanzas he repeated two, three, or even four times before he went on to the next. Perhaps these were the stanzas he liked or knew best. Whenever he began a stanza that was known by the people, many men and practically all the women who were awake fell in and sang with him.

Now he sang the second stanza and all the women inside the hut, including the pump-master woman, took up the song, at first hesitatingly but after a while with full voices. At times only one man sang because the others were rolling a new cigarette or greasing their throats from the bottle. Some got tired of singing and talked on without being disturbed by those who preferred the song.

The ragged peasant, however, sang all the time. He refused to take a swallow from the bottle which was offered him every once in a while. He was an agrarista and thought himself a communist. In his hut in the little village where he lived he had a little house-altar with a picture of the Holy Virgin in the middle and on one side a picture of Saint John and on the other side a little picture of Lenin, who he believed sat next to the throne of the Lord like Saint John and all the other saints. His demands from communism, like those of all the other agraristas in the republic, would be fully satisfied the moment he was given from ten to twenty acres of fairly good land free and with the assurance that it would never be taken away from him or his family. He was the kind who makes you wise about politics and makes you believe that communism can be boiled down to one simple formula: give men food, plenty of it, and assure them that they will always have a job. Keep the bellies well filled and provide lots of movies, admission one cent, and there will be no more preaching from soap boxes and never any talk about a revolution.

The singer was paid by no one. He sang out of pure love for the bereaved mother, to help her get over her loss without too many scars. The kid would be buried without the blessings of a priest and without a death certificate from a doctor. Priest and doctor cost money. Even if all the mourners contributed half the money they possessed they could not raise enough to meet such expenses. Moreover the burial could not wait two days. Despite the fact that the night was cool, the body had already started to decompose.

The agrarista sang only church hymns. But nobody who knew Roman Catholic hymns would ever think that these songs were really church hymns. Perhaps Catholics used to sing that way when the first monks came wandering through these jungles to bring the true faith to the poor pagans of the Americas. But whatever the original tunes might have been like, they had since been blended with worldly songs, including American dance melodies of more recent times. Once a year, or once in two years, the people might go to church and listen to a real hymn, and a little of it would remain in their memory. And then there were the dances in the settlements and villages where the musicians brought new tunes which had been picked up in the nearest large town, where they were considered the latest hits just arrived direct from Broadway, while in fact in New York no one could remember them any more, because they must have been crooned about the time when the best-dressed American was running for mayor. And so here in the jungle after each dance new tunes were added and the former ones were dropped as obsolete. Moreover, the uneducated Indian couldn't and wouldn't sing the way we think songs should be sung. In all their songs there was a certain pagan motif and frequently an almost savage one, which seemed to be a heritage from their forebears. In their hymns, sung without any accompaniment, save perhaps the beating of high drums and the plaintive sound of a home-made clarinet, this strange native motif was often so strong that it carried the whole tune and left hardly ten notes of the original hymn.

This funeral singer was known far and wide in the whole jungle region. He was considered the best of his kind and everybody admired him. He was their movie star and radio crooner all in one, because on other occasions, at weddings or at Saints'-day festivals, he sang corridos—that is, native ballads. He could not sing corridos as well as the professionals who visit the ferias and who bring to the people who cannot read newspapers the news of the latest political events and love tragedies in the form of ballads sung in the open places. As a funeral singer, however, this agrarista was far better than any of the corrido singers.

The greatest ambition of all the boys in that jungle region was to become a railroad man, as this was the highest position in the world they could think of and was certainly far higher than working for an oil company. But when the agrarista came and sang his hymns the boys changed their ambition and wished to be nothing better than a funeral singer as great and as famous as the agrarista.

When the first stanza had started, the Garcia, in her hut, screamed as if she were going mad. The women around her took her in their arms and kissed her. She grew quiet and only sobbed after a while. But when other men and women joined the singer and the whole yard was filled with the voices of the visitors, she was again overwhelmed by her grief. She fell into a terrible rage and with both her fists she hammered her skull. Grasping her hair, she pulled it so fiercely that the scalp

161

seemed about to be torn off. Suddenly she threw the whole weight of her body upon the table, which answered with threatening cracking sounds. Two men jumped close and held the legs of the table straight. Over and over again she threw her body upon her baby. Had he been alive she would have crushed his ribs, so violent was her outburst. And she yelled: "Chico mio, my little beloved! My sweet only baby! Why? Why did you go and leave your poor mother alone? Why? Why? Oh, Holy Mother of the Lord, why did you do this to me? Why? Why?" Whereupon she began to swear in the most horrible manner, cursing all the saints in heaven and the devil in hell. With her fists she hammered upon the kid's chest as if she meant to punish him for what he had done to her. When she did this a man seized her, dragged her back from the table, pushed back her head so that her mouth was straight up, and with his other hand grabbed a mescal-bottle. He forced the mouth of the bottle between her teeth, pushing the bottle in so that she could not turn away from it. She refused to take the brandy and struggled against both man and bottle. But another man went behind her and pressed her arms down, so that now she was defenseless. After that she got her mouth so full of that aguardiente that she could not help swallowing it in big gulps. The man did not let go until the bottle was nearly empty.

This medicine, however, was of little use. The woman didn't even get dull from the drink. And whenever she again became aware of the people singing hymns, she again got wild.

The women inside the hut could no longer resist the temptation to sing also, and so they fell in with the crowd singing in the yard. That caused the Garcia to shriek more than ever. Her crying was so loud and penetrating that for many minutes it drowned the voices of the singing women inside. Then she got weak and had to calm down. The women went on singing, considering it their duty to do so whether the mother spoiled

162

the hymns by her yelling or not. The Lord would forgive the mother for her almost sacrilegious behavior.

By now the mescal which had been poured into the Garcia began to show some effect. She was getting a bit foggy. Stroking back her hair, she glanced around and tried to remember what had happened. With blank eyes she looked at the women and apparently wondered what these people were doing here, how they came to be here, and what they wanted. She made a gesture as if she were going to say: "Out of here, all of you! Get out of my house and leave me alone!" Then she shrugged her shoulders as if to say: "What do I care? Let them stay here; perhaps they have no place to go while it is still night." She turned to the table and gazed at the body, and then she said: "Who is that kid, anyway?" The women stopped singing.

Hardly had she spoken thus when her whole body jerked. She blew her nose with a gesture of anger. Now she said in a very low voice: "Oh, my little baby, why didn't you wait for me? We would have crossed the bridge all right had you only waited and let me take you by your hand."

She looked at the women, who had stopped singing, and said: "It's in fun, isn't it? Say it's all in fun, please say it." No one answered.

The pump-master woman rose from her knees, took the Garcia woman in her arms, kissed her, and murmured: "Don't be that way, Carmelita, you'll soon have another one. God will send you one right from heaven."

Through her sobs the Garcia answered: "Don't say so, woman, I never wish to have another one in all my life. I'll kill it before it ever comes to light." She wept bitterly and said to the pump-master woman: "Forgive me, comadre, I didn't mean to say that. You see, here in my heart there is so much pain. I really don't know what I am saying. The kid pained me so much when he came, and now it pains a hundred thousand

163

times more when he goes. Forgive me, please. Tomorrow it will be different. It's only now, tonight, that I can't get over it. Only a few hours ago he was shouting and laughing and running, and now look what is left of him. And only a few hours." She sobbed on the breast of the pump-master woman.

If the singing stopped for a while, the cracking of the fireworks outside reminded the Garcia anew that the kid was awaited by the angels. She never got a chance to forget.

The singing, when it was a new entertainment, had aroused the people, but now it had lost its attraction; everyone got sleepier than before. Many threw themselves flat on the ground. Others squatted, embraced their knees, and put their heads on them and then fell asleep immediately. A few men and women stayed awake, not because they were not sleepy but because there was still something left in the bottles—and it is an old saying that he who sleeps cannot drink.

Inside the hut the women were no less weary and sleepy than the people in the yard. Two women had already taken possession of the corrupted shakedown which the Garcias called their bed. Fully dressed, they lay there snoring like soldiers after a battle.

The little fire on the floor of the hut smoldered lazily. If it had been a cat it would surely have yawned. A few pots were standing close to it. Nobody cared what they were for, what was in them, or who had set them by the fire. Nobody asked. Indeed, nobody seemed to be interested in anything. Sleep, or at least the desire to sleep, ruled the scene.

28

 During the past half-hour the agrarista had sung with difficulty. He had become hoarse. All who were still awake shuffled about and tried to sneak out of the hut without hurting the Garcia's feelings. Some were talking just to keep awake.

The agrarista and the men who had come with him entered the hut. They looked at the kid for the last time. They shook hands with the mother and told her again how sorry they were and then praised her for being so brave.

The Garcia said to each one of them: "Muchas, muchas gracias, señor! Vaya con Dios! The Lord be with you on your way home! I thank you for your visit and for the beautiful songs you have sung in honor of my baby. Adiós, señores!"

When the last of these men had gone, the Garcia remained standing limply and stared vacantly at the door. The men went to their horses and, with many loud adioses, rode off. The Garcia still gazed after them.

The misty gown of the new day slowly descended upon the earth. Millions of pearls gleamed on the grass, on the leaves of the trees, and in the folds of the flowers, all of which were awaiting the kiss of the sun. Then the morning breeze dissolved the mist, and the new day was born.

The Garcia shivered in the cool morning wind. She went to the door and ran her eyes over the crowd sleeping in the yard. She felt alone and forgotten.

A golden spark leaped into the air from beyond the prairie. It seemed but a moment later that the sun rose over the jungle.

The Garcia turned around and saw that her hut was filled with daylight, in which the smoking, flickering candles looked ghostly. Although the daylight entered the hut only through the open door, it changed the whole interior, leaving nothing in it untouched.

The light of the few candles had been unable to reach the corners of the hut and so everything which otherwise would have looked ugly had been mercifully hidden. The home had not been without a certain beauty—like that of a very poor chapel—but the daylight destroyed the illusion. The hut now looked gloomy and unpleasant.

The Garcia's face was haggard and swollen from so much weeping; her eyes were dry, dull, and inflamed and they were sunk in deep black hollows. She looked like a wax mask carved by an insane sculptor. She was still wearing her green gauze dress. The flowers at her girdle were torn and withered. The flowers in her hair had fallen long before. At night the dress had seemed quite becoming, but now it looked as if it did not belong to her. It only followed her, but was not worn by her. The woman was still the mother of the kid, but the dress no longer covered the mother. It was a stained, ugly corpse of a dress which trailed after her wherever she went.

The kid, who had been a very beautiful sight at night, was now an ordinary carcass—a carcass dressed up in a monkey suit. His mouth was green, and matter was running out of his smashed jaw. The strings which held his hands together were

166

cutting deep scars into his wrists. His little folded hands looked as if they had been tied together by a professional tormentor.

The rays of the sun came like spears through the sticks of the walls.

The Garcia saw the rays touch the body. For the first time she now saw what all the others had seen long ago, that her baby was gone, was no longer with her in the hut. The little heap of flesh lying on the table could no longer be kissed. The morning breeze, blowing through the walls and coming in through the door, brought the odor of death to her nostrils. She shuddered, turned away from her child, and moaned in despair.

When she looked at him again she noticed that big green flies were beginning to settle on the body. She hurried to pick up a piece of cloth to cover the little face. But after that she could look no more at her child.

Luckily for her, she had no time to sit down and brood over things which could not be undone. For with the new day a great number of new visitors had arrived and more were expected. The news of the drowning and the miraculous discovery of the body had spread. No sooner did the people hear the story than they mounted their burros, mules, or horses and left home to visit the unhappy mother, to tell her that everybody loved her dearly and that whoever had a soul and a heart was weeping with her. Since it was Sunday it was easy for people to come, and the crowd was growing bigger with every half-hour.

The men dismounted, helped their womenfolk and children off the animals, tied the animals to posts, trees, or shrubs or let them roam on their own, rolled cigarettes, and started talking to the other men.

The women, one after another, entered the hut. Here they greeted the mother, embraced her, kissed her, and then looked at the little body. Their eyes became wet. The Garcia shrieked: "Why did this have to happen? Why, tell me, why? Isn't there any longer a God in heaven?"

She took the cloth off the face so that the newcomers could look at the kid. Although they were terribly shocked on seeing the ugly face, they suppressed their feelings, and invariably they said: "He looks beautiful! Such a sweet little angel he is now! Doesn't he look sweet and beautiful?" And the other women answered: "Yes, indeed, he is a little angel, un angelito muy lindo."

Many of the women now arriving brought armfuls of flowers; others brought wreaths hastily made of twigs and covered with gold and silver paper. They put the flowers and wreaths aside without mentioning their gifts so as to spare the Garcia the pain of thanking them. These poor people, so very sincere in their sympathies, did not know the custom of the civilized of putting engraved cards on their flowers so that the family would know who gave what and who gave nothing, and so that the names of the mourners might be properly spelled when they were printed in the social columns. Here no one cared who brought flowers or other gifts and who did not. If one did not give something it was because he had nothing to give. But he was honored just as much as those who had brought things. Whatever the visitors, the mourners, the neighbors did, they did out of pure love for the mother.

"Yes," repeated a woman, "yes, it is true he looks beautiful, the little Carlosito does, just like an angel, only with his wings not fully grown yet." Another one said: "To tell the truth, I've never in all my life seen such a beautiful little boy."

The Garcia woman had already heard the praise. But she was a woman even in sorrow; she waited for more praise. She stopped her sobbing, grasped the hands of all the women around her, and said: "Muchas gracias! O mil, mil gracias for your kindness. You women make me so very happy, very, very happy, thank you ever so much!"

168

She meant it because she was really grateful for the admiration rendered her dolled-up baby and she accepted the approval as if it were given for something she herself had achieved.

The exclamations of the women were not empty flattery. They praised the kid partly out of an inborn courtesy, but to some extent they felt as they said they did. To them the little prince with the golden crown on his head and the golden scepter in his hand was something quite beautiful. He reminded them of the crowned little Jesus child held in the arms of His Holy Mother, which they saw in church and knelt before in prayer.

All the visitors were unbelievably poor. The women who had just arrived were barefooted. Their bodies were covered with thin, worn-out cotton dresses that were full of holes. The thorns take no pity on the poverty of an Indian woman who has to ride through the jungle. They wore black gauze shawls on their heads to protect them against the sun.

Most of the women had brought their babies with them. Sitting by the corpse, they pulled down their dresses and gave their babies to drink. At the same time they wept and sobbed. At intervals they interrupted their lamentations to blow their noses and ask the Garcia how it had happened and how the kid had been found.

The Garcia had covered the kid's face right after the last woman had paid him her respects.

Staying in the hut was becoming a real torture as the sun rose higher. The stench of death was making breathing difficult. Two women with child got pale and had to be led out to recover. The smoking candles, the heavy perfume around the masses of flowers which were dying so painfully and which refused to die so soon, the drifting smoke produced by the bonfire outside, the smell of mescal, coffee, and tobacco, and the odor of the many unwashed men and women crowded in that small hut, all this thick, almost suffocating air accumulated under the grass roof and could not drift away. But the people stayed there, out of politeness and out of respect for the suffering mother.

In two hours the morning breeze would cease. After that, until eleven in the morning, there would be not even the slightest bit of wind. By that time the interior of the hut would resemble a furnace in which a carcass had been burned. But whatever happened and no matter how unbearable the air in the hut might become, as long as the Garcia stayed inside, all the others would stay too.

The men who had come with the women and who were still outside had finished their cigarettes. They took their hats off and entered the hut. They came like frightened little boys late for school. One went to the body and took the piece of cloth away from the face. All the men came close, gazed at the corpse, stood around for two minutes, and left again. It appeared they were not sure whether they should shake hands with the mother or ask her how it had happened or talk to her about nothing in particular or keep silent altogether. But the fact was that none was really embarrassed. These people were very seldom or never embarrassed. Their behavior was determined by one thought only: what to do to make the mother forget her loss. So in this case they had decided not to shake hands with the mother and not to ask questions which they were sure the mother had had to answer a hundred times already and they had also decided not even to tell the mother how beautiful they thought the baby looked. His mother knew that well enough. That was the reason they kept silent, and by so doing they were convinced that they had shown best their deep sympathy for the mother.

Whatever these people did or said, nothing was a cold formula which had been taught them. It all came out of their hearts. Their hearts were speaking, their hearts were ordering them to go on a long trip to console the mother, their hearts

170

were commanding them to be silent when they felt it showed deeper sympathy to be silent. On leaving his host none would say: "I've had a lovely time," if he did not feel that way. In such a case he would rather say: "Sorry, I think I've got to beat it now, for work is waiting back home. I hope to see you soon in my humble house, which is yours and where you're welcome whenever it pleases you to come."

This knowledge of their good taste and of their delicate tact when meeting their fellow men had come to me bit by bit during the past twelve hours through observing them and taking notice of all their doings and sayings. When I had first come here, I had seen in these people the simple Indian peasants with ordinary courtesy such as one might find all over Spanish America in places where American tourists had never come to ruin the landscapes and try to make natives understand how glorious civilization is and tell them ten times a day how dirty and filthy they are and how badly organized their country is. It seemed that an occasion such as the one I had witnessed was necessary if one wanted to see those people as they really were, to see not only their dirt and their rags, but, what was more, their hearts and souls, the only things in man which count. Radios, Fords, and speed records do not count at all; they are but garbage when it comes to the final balance sheet.

It is religion that makes men love their neighbors and that dries the tears of a mother who has lost her baby and that makes you who have two shirts give one to the poor who has nothing with which to cover his nakedness. Is it religion? Death is usually an occasion for lip religion to show off in all its splendor. And here, where death marched silently into a gay party all set for a merry week-end of dancing, I could not see a glimpse of the white man's great religion. I had heard no prayers so far. Nobody had fingered a rosary. The singing of hymns by the communist agrarista was only very superficially

171

connected with the Catholic religion because his singing had the eternal worldly meaning of good will to all men, and the Holy Virgin was called upon merely to inform her of what was happening, not to come down and help a poor Indian mother out of her sorrows. And it was because religion as we understand it had not entered either the hearts or the inner minds of these people that they could preserve hearts and souls overflowing with kindness and love.

I was sitting on a box a few feet from the door. Whoever came in or went out had plenty of room to pass by without disturbing me in the least. Nevertheless everybody, man, woman, or youngster, who passed stopped in front of me and said: "With your kind permission, señor!" And only after I had answered: "Pase!" or "Es su propio!" would he go out or enter. He did not do so because I was a white man. If an Indian peasant in rags had been sitting on this box, all the people passing by him would just as seriously have asked his permission to do so. To them it was impossible to cut through the breath of a human being without having his permission to do so. Of course, I did the same thing when passing an Indian. Suppose I should be as courteous back home as I was here; everybody would believe I had come home with a tropical disease. Back home I bleat exactly as do all the other sheep. I know it is easier on the nerves if you don't try to lift people up to your own standard and it makes you only yellow in the face or gives you high blood-pressure to insist on reforming people who are convinced that they know better than anybody else what is good for them. One becomes a philosopher by living among people who are not of his own race and who speak a different language. No, no matter what happens, you had better stay firm in the belief that there is no better country in the world than God's own great land of the free and then you will feel fine and be a respected citizen. Aside from the fact that that philosophy actually pays if you know

172

how to handle it right, experience has taught me that traveling educates only those who can be educated just as well by roaming around their own country. By walking thirty miles anywhere in one's home state the man who is open minded will see more and learn more than a thousand others will by running round the world. A trip to a Central American jungle to watch how Indians behave near a bridge won't make you see either the jungle or the bridge or the Indians if you believe that the civilization you were born into is the only one that counts. Go and look around with the idea that everything you learned in school and college is wrong.

29

 As I was feeling hungry I went to see what Sleigh was doing.

The girl had long been up. She had ground the boiled corn on the metate, toasted tortillas, cooked black beans, and set the coffee on the fire.

"Coffee isn't ready yet," Sleigh said the minute he saw me. "We'll have to wait a quarter of an hour or so. It would be different if my wife was here. Hell, I'm sleepy. Christ, I should say, I am damn sleepy, that's what I am."

He dozed off. Right away he was awake again and asked me: "Haven't you seen the boy? I mean that lazy stick that works with me. He has to carry the milk to the store."

"He is at the fire helping the half-wit along with the fireworks."

"So that's where he is. I'll kick him in the pants. He knows he has to attend to the milk or it will turn sour in that blazing sun before he gets it to the store." He rose from his seat and both of us walked back to the Garcia's.

On arriving at the yard we saw Garcia returning from his mysterious trip.

174

Out of his bast bag dangling from the saddle horn he took a bundle of candles, a package of oily ground coffee, four cones of crude brown sugar, and three quart bottles of mescal. One of the bottles was half empty. Of course, there was a good excuse for that. The way was long, and he was heart-broken, old man Garcia was. So there was nothing to wonder at that he had such brilliance in his eyes. His face was red and had a spongy appearance. He was honest and did not pretend to be sober. Right away the bottle was handed to the friend who was holding the horse while he dismounted. The friend took a shot and then the bottle went the rounds.

When he had arrived at the general store, Garcia had had only a few pesos in his pocket, but because of his sad loss the storekeeper had been willing to charge what he needed for the funeral. Garcia would have felt humiliated if he had had to celebrate the funeral of his son without mescal, coffee, sugar, and sufficient candles. The storekeeper knew, of course, that while other debts might be difficult to collect, the expenses incurred on account of the funeral would be paid as soon as Garcia had the money. As all prices at this general store were more than twice as high as in the town stores, the storekeeper would make an excellent profit out of this sale; in fact, the cash Garcia had paid amounted to practically four-fifths of the storekeeper's costs for these goods. As elsewhere, no battlefield is so sad and horrible that some men cannot make a good profit out of it. Everything under heaven can be turned to dollars or pesos. It really does not matter whether it is the tears of a mother or the laughter of a child or the sufferings of the poor, there is always money in it. Man has to pay for his grief as well as for his joys, for his stumblings as well as for his dances. Even his last little cave under the ground, where he no longer will be in anybody's way, has to be paid for, or he goes into the ashcan, unless a kind student of medicine takes pity on him and relieves him of such a shameless finale. Were it not so, the world would be a lot less entertaining.

"Muchacho!" Sleigh shouted. "What about the milk?"

"Estoy volando, jefe, I am flying already," the boy yelled back.

"Hurry up! And no maybe from your lips. Señor Velasquez will beat the hell out of you if you bring him sour milk."

In spite of his harsh words Sleigh was not a bit worried or angry about what might happen to the few quarts of milk, and he was still less concerned about what Señor Velasquez might say or do. Señor Velasquez was the owner of the general store in a village located near the depot. Should Señor Velasquez complain about the milk when Sleigh visited him to check the accounts and collect the money that had to be sent to the owner of the ranch, Sleigh would lend a deaf ear to him. He would turn his back to him, mount his horse, and ride back home. If Sleigh loved anything at all, it was the cattle he was in charge of, but he did not care a rap about his boss, or about Señor Velasquez, or about the milk. In his opinion it was only incidentally that his boss or Señor Velasquez or the milk had anything to do with the cattle.

We returned to Sleigh's hut to breakfast on an old kerosene box. A not very clean newspaper served as a tablecloth.

Sleigh looked the table over as if something were missing from it. He then said to the girl: "Fry each of us another coupla eggs."

"Si, patrón, ahorititq!" the girl answered.

She went to a dark corner of the hut where a basket was tied to the post which supported the roof. A sleepy-eyed hen was sitting comfortably in this basket, obviously brooding over nature's whim which made her sit there while all the other hens could go about and wink at the rooster. The girl snatched the hen by the neck, threw her out of the basket, picked up four eggs, and returned with them to the hearth. The hen cackled noisily and ran around the hut violently. She jumped on our table, kicked over our coffee cups, flew up, glided down again, and ran back to her basket, where for a while she sat on the edge and looked inside. Then she hopped in, moved the eggs around, counted them with her claws, and, finding none missing, sat down quietly and closed her eyes, once more satisfied with the world. She was happy and satisfied with everything on earth because she could not count correctly. It is the ability to count correctly that causes so many tragedies among men. Since counting-machines have made mistakes practically impossible, tragedies resulting from counting have become more intense and greater in number.

After we had had our breakfast, we thought it time to get some sleep.

30

 Music awoke me. The two musicians who should have been here last night and who, if they had come then, might not now be needed to play for the funeral, were presenting a lively foxtrot as an introduction.

Sleigh had arisen long ago. He was crawling through the brush because a calf had broken out of the corral. I washed up, shaved, gulped down two cups of hot coffee, swallowed a few spoonfuls of beans wrapped in hot tortillas, and then went over to the Garcia's.

Here I found a great and animated assembly. To every tree, shrub, or post a horse, a mule, or a burro was tied—some with the saddle still on, others without. Women dressed in their Sunday garments, men clothed as on week-days were standing around or squatting on the ground. A crowd of children filled the air with shouts and shrieks. Most of them were naked, the rest half naked, the latter being mostly girls.

More fireworks had been brought by the new visitors and there was a cracking and shooting and a tremendous noise all over the place.

178

The musicians who had played the whole night through were now no longer playing. They preserved their strength for the long march through the bush to the cemetery.

A few men were lying about drunk. Others were still sleeping here and there on the ground. Nobody disturbed them.

The sun was high and blazed down without mercy. The drunks caught in this broiling heat became uneasy, woke up, crawled to the shade, and fell back into stupor. One or two failed to reach the shade, dropped, and remained lying like shapeless bundles.

Goats and hogs were running around freely and getting in the way of the people, who kicked them and pushed them without any result. A multitude of dogs were constantly fighting each other or playing or chasing the hogs. Chickens were fighting with turkeys over worms and crumbs of food. The horses, burros, and mules which were not tied up or which had freed themselves were walking among the crowd looking for a green leaf which had not yet been trodden into the ground. Yesterday there was much green to be seen near the broken-down fence and in the corners of the yard. Now the soil looked as if locusts had passed over it.

All these animals were a nuisance to the people, but nobody got seriously angry over the annoyances they caused. Now and then an animal would be kicked. A woman would shout: "Hi, you perro, you miserable dog, get away!" Another: "Hog, don't push me down!" Occasionally a boy was called to chase a dog or a hog away. Or a stone would be thrown, but so gently that it could not hurt the animal. It was meant to be only a warning, not a punishment. But if a dog or a hog was fresh enough to try to get away with the whole morral, the little bast bag in which the family carried their provisions for the trip, a club or a big stone thrown at the thief would remind him to have more respect for other people's property.

179

Some groups were all laughter. Other groups entertained themselves with animated conversation. Groups of youngsters sang and played mouth-organs. Here and there men were appraising horses and mules. Some women were telling others about the troubles they had with their children or with their relatives or their neighbors. It wasn't all love and kindness. They told how greedy a sister-in-law was or an uncle, and what a beastly neighbor Don Chucho was.

Any outsider who had come along here at this time would never have thought for a minute that the assembly was there for a funeral. But now and then people were reminded of the fact and they became serious as befitted the situation. At such moments groups suddenly ceased being jolly or loud. Someone would then say: "Well, all of us have to die some day, one sooner, another later, and some will die before they are out of their babyhood. That's only natural. Poor mother! She'll have to bear it and live on." And a sigh from all the women in this group confirmed the truth of that philosophical statement.

Again, in another group which had become too noisy, a man's voice would be heard saying: "Get quiet, all of you! You ought to be ashamed of yourself making such a row and laughing as if you'd burst. Don't you know that there is a dead baby close by, and that woman crying out her guts? You've not got a bit of decency left, that's what I say."

In many places blankets had been spread over sticks planted in the ground so as to make little roofs for protection against the sun. There were few trees in the yard big enough to give any real shade.

Usually a fresh breeze would come up at about eleven in the morning. Today this breeze had failed to come.

Now the shadows of humans, animals, trees, and posts were right at their feet and could hardly be noticed at all.

I took off my hat and entered the hut to see what changes had taken place.

180

The hut was crowded with women who were fanning themselves with pieces of cardboard and with fans made of paste-
board on which were printed advertisements of cigarettes,
beer, tequila, habanero, and dry-goods stores, and kissing
couples with titles of moving pictures. The women fanned
themselves automatically, as if their hands were moved by a
little machine.

All candles were bent and at every candle a woman worked
to keep it upright. This constant attention to the candles not
only kept a number of women and youngsters very busy, but
also served as a good show for the mourners, because each
candle had its individuality and each attendant had a different
way of handling the candle she was in charge of.

The kid had become a very poor side-show and was not
attracting any real interest.

Then the Garcia once again took the cloth off the kid's face.
The face could no longer be recognized. It had become almost
formless. The wound in his jaw had become an enormous ugly
opening. His teeth were exposed like those of a skeleton. The
gums were greenish. The little wound on his skull had also
widened and the bared bone of the skull had become visible.

It was not only the tropical climate that accounted for such
rapid destruction; the process was also hastened by the water
from the tropical river which had entered the body. The
water of a river in the tropics contains billions of the most
hungry, most voracious microbes, which attack a lifeless body
a hundred times more savagely than those which infest water
in the temperate zones. I for one could explain in no other way
such a terrific and horrible decomposition in so short a time. I
wondered what the body looked like under the sailor suit.

But the sailor suit was no longer visible. These primitive
women had perceived the ugliness of that monkey dress. They
had better taste than the jobber who had shipped a gross of
these suits down here in the belief that they were the right

clothes for little Indian boys who lived in the jungle where nobody knew what a ship looked like and where nobody understood why sailors had to wear this sort of suit and why they could not do their work just as efficiently in overalls. Of course, intelligent people know that it is the uniform that accounts for a good sailor's smooth and effective work. But while this may be known to the women in every port in the world, it is not known to the people in a tropical jungle.

The women had covered the admiral's overalls with a sort of frock made of red, green, blue, and yellow paper. This frock which had been made by simple Indian women had given back to the little Indian boy his dignity. I was surprised to see at least a dozen identical frocks on the kid. Soon I found the reason for this unnecessary abundance.

Almost every woman had brought something with her to be used for dolling up the kid. There was no possibility of exchanging ideas over the phone before leaving their homes. Many had brought a dozen sheets of colored paper. Others had made paper frocks as soon as they had received the news of the tragedy. Since every woman had offered her gift with all her sympathy and love, the mother accepted them all with thanks and, with the assistance of each giver, dressed the kid in the new frock even though he had more than one on already.

Fortunately, not all the women had brought frocks. Many offered little stars and crosses, some of them cut out of tin cans, others out of colored paper. These stars and crosses were pasted on the uppermost frock as extra decorations. A few women who had nothing better to give had brought brightly colored rags and ribbons, which were also pinned to the frock.

A woman I knew entered. She was the mother of the boy whom I would have raised from the dead but for the Spaniard pushing me aside and applying another method. I was still pondering over the question whether I would be as highly respected today in that village if the Spaniard had not inter-

182

fered with my handling of the dead. Well, perhaps the people of that village would admire me just the same, because working on a corpse with all sorts of rescue methods for six consecutive hours will always be highly appreciated even if the result is failure.

That woman greeted me before anyone else, and she did so in a very friendly manner. She had brought a pretty crown made of gold paper, but it had not been made with such good taste as the one made by the pump-master woman last night. She naturally believed, however, that her crown was lots prettier than the one the kid already had on his head. She stepped up to the body, and without asking anybody's permission she took off the old crown and put on the crown she had made.

The pump-master woman saw her do this, but did not interfere. When she had made that crown, with her tears running down over it, I had noticed how much kindness, neighborly love, and compassion for another mother in distress she had been weaving into it, and I also saw how happy she had felt when she had finished her job and examined it with the satisfaction of an artist whose work has surpassed his intentions. I shall never forget the look in her smiling eyes, still wet from tears, when she put that crown on the kid's head and almost worshiped him as if he had now become a little saint.

Now she glanced at her rival and for a moment I was not sure that a fight might not start. She made a gesture as if she meant to prevent the unceremonious exchange of crowns. But she stopped, and over her lips a kind smile fluttered. She put both her hands over her breasts and watched the somewhat rude exchange without anger. Being a mother, she perhaps realized that the other woman was also a mother and that only recently that mother had lost a beloved son and what she was doing at this moment was but showing her sympathy for the young mother. And so, the pump-master woman thought, why start a fight over the crowns? The first crown had served its purpose, so let the second crown have its turn.

The woman with the new crown had thrown the old one aside as if to say: Well, what sort of junk is that? The pump-master woman picked up her discarded crown, crumpled it in her hand so that nobody would pay any attention to it, left the hut, and threw it into the bonfire.

31

 Suddenly excited voices were heard outside the hut.
Right away a man entered carrying under one arm
the little coffin which he himself had made as his last gift to
the kid. With his free hand he took off his hat.

The moment he put the coffin on the floor the Garcia
woman broke out into a fit of hysterical shrieking. All the
other women in the hut and outside in the yard joined her as if
they were all mad.

The coffin-maker wiped the thick sweat off his forehead
with the backs of his hands and then dried his neck with a
large red handkerchief.

Three men came in and went straight to the table. The
Garcia woman yelled: "Don't take him away from me! Let
him sleep here only a few hours more, please, don't take him
away!" She wrung her hands and ran around the hut, pushing
her head here and there against the posts which supported the
roof, shrieking and yelling all the time. Finally two women
cornered her and took her in their arms.

In the meantime, with a short businesslike "Con su per-

185

miso!" and ignoring the shrieks and lamentations of the women, the men pushed the women out of their way and got to work.

Sleigh was one of the three who had just come in.

The coffin was only a very crude box made of rotten boards taken from different kinds of old cases. Not a bit of this coffin was planed. The outside was covered with blue and red paper to give it a more decent appearance. The inside had been filled with dry grass and corn leaves, on top of which pieces of limestone had been laid.

The coffin was set on a box. Without any ceremony the four men grabbed the little body and tried to lift it from the table. While lifting it the head dropped with a jerk as if it would break off. I jumped forward and held the pillow under it for support. The beautiful paper dresses spread apart and the whole laboriously achieved make-up turned into something horrible. But at last we got the body into the coffin. The pump-master woman jumped up and with her quick, expert hands arranged the dresses to give back the body its former illusion of beauty.

The coffin was then put on the table. At once the Garcia threw herself over her baby to kiss him good-by. She was just about to press her lips to his mouth when she realized that his lips were all gone. Then she smelled the odor rising from the poor little body. She gasped for fresh air and drew back, almost falling over the woman sitting there.

She stood five feet away from her baby. She flung her arms up, waved them violently, then dropped them with a gesture of fatigue. Now her hands fumbled at her face, ran up and down her breasts, and finally glided down her belly, where she moved them around as if she were searching for something hidden there. Then her fingers climbed up her face like little snakes until they reached her hair. She pulled at her hair so savagely that two women fell into her arms to keep her from

186

tearing her scalp off. Her eyes flickered about helplessly. She broke away from them, screamed, and dropped to the floor as if she had been struck by a club.

The women lifted her head, poured water between her tightly pressed lips, and tried to force open her clenched fists. First her lips and then her face got blue—but only for a minute. Slowly she came to. She opened her eyes, sat up on the floor, wiped her face, looked around, recognized her friends, and tried to smile at them.

That was her last good-by to her beloved baby.

Her husband came in. Staggering towards her, he dragged out of one of his pockets, with great difficulty, a bottle of mescal and pushed it into her hands with a gesture of love and sympathetic understanding.

The Garcia, holding the bottle in her hands as if it were something very sacred, rose from the floor and disappeared into the little storeroom. I could watch her through the sticks which formed the wall and I saw her take a swig which would have knocked an old Norwegian sailor straight under the table. She took the bottle from her mouth, looked at it, and then took a shot that was not quite so big as the first one, but was still more than two fingers of a quart bottle. Having taken her consoling medicine, she came out and, good and honest wife that she was, returned the bottle to her lord and master. She wiped her mouth with the back of her hand with a satisfied look in her hollow eyes.

Since the bottle was out of his hip pocket and since it had been so hard to get it out, old man Garcia thought the occasion very opportune and he too whipped a fine shot down his throat. Fiestas must be celebrated on the day they fall.

The coffin-maker dragged a hammer out of one pocket and out of another two thick rusty nails. He considered this gesture more suggestive than a speech about what he was now going to do.

187

The Garcia immediately understood the meaning of that gesture. She went up to the coffin, took off the cloth, and looked at what was still left of the face which had only yesterday been so full of life and joy. She stared in horror and covered the face hastily.

She stood there for a minute as if she were waiting for something. Then she walked with quick steps to the little shelf on which the picture of the Holy Virgin was standing, removed the little ukulele, and put it in the coffin beside the kid. Then she pondered again over something she wanted to remember. Once more she returned to the shelf, gathered together all of the kid's playthings—the battered tin automobile, the fish-hook, the strings, the broken cork, and the few other silly items which her boy had treasured so highly—carried them to the coffin, and put them in too. And in a very low voice she said: "He mustn't feel lonely, he mustn't." And after standing there a few seconds more, she said: "Adiós, Carlitos! Adiós, Carlosito mio!"

Nobody in the hut moved, nobody said a word, nobody mumbled, nobody even seemed to breathe while the mother was talking to her baby.

She bowed her head, turned around until her back was to the coffin, and walked towards the wall through which she could see the bonfire outside.

Quickly the coffin-maker put the lid on the box and with a few light blows of his hammer nailed it loosely so that it could be taken off again before the burial.

32

 From now on, everything happened in a hurry. Four youngsters, each about fourteen years of age, lifted the coffin, and the funeral train was on its way.

Men, women, children followed the pall-bearers. The women carried their babies on their backs wrapped in rebozos.

In no time the train had reached the spot on the bridge from which the kid was supposed to have tumbled over.

Here the pall-bearers instinctively halted.

All the men took off their hats. The Garcia wept bitterly, but she did not yell. Her tears stirred the hearts of all the mourners more than her yells had, honest though they had been. The pump-master woman kissed her. "There, there, now," she said, "weep if it helps you. Here, blow your nose in this." The pump-master woman pressed her handkerchief against the mother's swollen face.

The pall-bearers marched on again.

Sleigh had stopped on the bridge with the others for a minute. Then he turned around and went home as soon as he saw the procession move on. He did not say so, but I was sure he had to find a cow which had strayed.

The crowd left the bridge and passed the pump-station. On this rough, occasionally swampy trail through the bush, it would take almost the whole afternoon for the procession to reach the little cemetery.

Naturally, the mourners did not march in good order.

Garcia staggered between two friends who had difficulty keeping him on his feet, especially since they themselves were no longer very sure of their faculties.

The mother walked beside the pump-master woman, on whose right arm she was hanging. She still wore her sea-green gauze dress and apparently she did not know it. Aside from her week-day rags she had nothing else to wear on such a great occasion. The dress was streaked with blood and mud. It had many holes in it and was ripped wide open at various places. The flowers had fallen off, but the safety pins by which they had been fastened were still there.

The pump-master woman, like practically all the other women, also wore the dress she had worn the night before, but her dress and those of the other women were less soiled and not torn.

After the people had left the bridge they all began to feel more comfortable. A new world opened before them and that sinister bridge would soon be forgotten.

After having walked in silence for a quarter of an hour, the crowd slowly began to get lively. A heavy burden seemed to have been removed from everyone's chest.

The musicians—one fiddler and one guitar-player, both Indians—lifted their instruments. They did not know that there were such things as funeral dirges, death marches, and nocturnos which allure ghosts to come out of their chimneys and attics and dance before a pleased audience. That hymns existed they knew because they had heard them in church. Yet they could not play them, and for some unexplainable reason they would not have played them even if they had known

190

how. What in the world were the American jazz compositions for if not to be played any time and on any occasion, whether a wedding, or a baptism, a saint's day, a dance, or a funeral? Music was music anywhere and to have different tunes for different occasions was silly and befitted only people who knew no better—perhaps because they had degenerated and needed a rough-fisted bolshevism to put them out of their misery. Be this as it may, the little boy had to be buried with music, and any music would do, since he was already on his way to heaven.

I was afraid that they might play something like *Home, Sweet Home* or *My Old Kentucky Home*. But no, these good Indian musicians were not that far away from the path of civilization. They were far nearer to us. I could see here very clearly that international borders and the colors of skins weren't barriers against the spread of our mighty culture. The dynamic force of our crooners, torch singers, and night-club hostesses had actually made it possible for our Vallees, Berlins, Whitemans, and Crosbys to reach even the depths of American jungles. Over this trail blazed by our dance songs, there would soon arrive Fords, vacuum cleaners, electric refrigerators, air-conditioned grass huts, jungle-colored bathrooms, windmill-driven television, canned alligator stew, and pulverized hearts of young palm trees.

So it was that the tune played (as befitted the sailor suit) was *Taintgonnarainnomo*, which was the latest around here.

It was a long time since I had heard that tune. And since the time that tune was the rage back home, we Americans, tough guys that we are, have happily survived weddings of painted dolls, sonnyboys, and mammies crooned by poor devils suffering from St. Vitus's dance; we had also had to swallow the strange news that only God can make a tree, a fact which none of us ever knew until we were told so by night-club entertainers. Then there was the coming (two hundred times every

191

day and night) of the moon over the mountains with my mem'ries of you. Then we took our sugar to tea, asked for just one more chance, and incorporated the little innocent cucaracha, which used to be sung by Mexican revolutionists under the fire of machine-guns, but was sung by us under the fire of booze.

Everything in its right place and the world will be a better location to live in. No, it won't rain any more. This elegant song was played by Indians who for nine months had had no drop of rain and by whom rain was considered God's greatest blessing.

We reach these people so easily with our sailor suits, with our polished shoes and our yeswehavenobananas. Would that we tried once in a while to reach them, not with puffed rice and naked celluloid dames going with the wrong man in the right bed, but with the Gettysburg address, which next to God's rain would be the greatest blessing to all these so-called republics if we would take the trouble to make the people understand the true meaning of the greatest, finest, and most noble poem any American has produced to this day.

Yet the simple fact that the taintgonnarainnomo tune was played here as a death march was ample proof that this vomit of our civilization had, at least in this part of the world, met a wall it could not break. Death is understood by these people, but the hypocrisy with which we, the followers of Christ, bury our dead they cannot understand. Therefore American dance tunes could not confuse their feelings, while hymns and nearer-to-thees would only upset them as something not quite befitting that great mystery which is the extinction of life.

What does it all matter anyhow? What does the sun above us care about the dead, about weeping mothers, about funerals, about American foxtrots and hair-removers? What does it care whether there is genuine culture or faked civilization, whether good music or noise with brass tubes? That glorious sun

192

doesn't give a rap for anybody's anger about the white man's dumping the contents of his ashcans over the heads of people he believes inferior. Whatever woe, pain, and sorrow we may have, real or imaginary, the sun stays mighty and dignified in the universe. It is a god, it is the only god, the redeemer, the savior, the only visible one, the always present, the ever young, the ever smiling god, forever an exulting song of eternal creation. It is the creator, the maintainer, the begetter, and the producer. It gives and wastes at the same time, never ceases to bless the earth with fruit and beauty, yet never asks for prayers or worship, nor for thanks. And it never threatens punishments.

What did the sun above us care about our funeral? It stood directly above and its flames struck us. We staggered along our dreary way, stumbled over roots and logs, fell into holes, and sank into swampy furrows. We squeezed ourselves through thorny brushes and beat our way through the high, wiry prairie grass.

For hours and hours we marched in this blazing heat. The crowd was chatting, laughing, yelling, squeaking, singing, whistling. Now and then the music played. Foxtrots, one-steps, two-steps, blues. Occasionally they played the *Jesusita en Chihuahua* and the *Reina de mi jacal* and *Amapola del camino* and *Adelita* for recreation, because these tunes they could play in their sleep. But if they had gone on playing these beautiful songs, the mourners would have believed them old-fashioned, and so that they should not be thought narrow-minded, doing only what their grandfathers did, they discarded their fine folk-music to show the crowd how Americanized they were. And there came floating through the boiling air the sounds of that musical glory of the century, the great American Te Deum, *Taintgonnarainnomo.*

The coffin swayed dangerously on the shoulders of the youngsters who carried it. If now and then one of them

193

tripped over a stone or a root or sank into a hole, the entire crowd yelled: "La caja, la caja! The box, the box!"

Those walking near it jumped closer and supported the case, for otherwise it might easily have gone down the scarp which bordered the trail. I did not wish even to imagine what might happen if that coffin had really gone down there and burst open.

On both sides of our trail buzzards accompanied us, some flying ahead of us, others following, some of them dropping into a tree or a bush to perch there for a minute, then arising again and coming close to us. They never came very close—just close enough so that we could clearly see their hungry eyes and their dry beaks.

We came up to a row of termite-eaten fence posts. From a few of them pieces of rusty barbed wire were dangling. A dozen buzzards took possession of this row and perched on the posts. It was a ghastly sight, considering that we were going to bury a dead child, for these buzzards sat in a file like sentinels. A mourner tried to make a wisecrack and remarked: "With their black frock coats they look like undertakers." Another one said with a giggle: "That one there looks exactly like our cura, who baptized our brats last fall."

I too thought they looked more like ministers than undertakers—like ministers who could never forgive an error and who were at their best when preaching of hell-fire and Satan's sadistic pleasures.

In front of the coffin the second brother marched. He was surrounded by a bunch of shouting and shrieking kids. One of the boys was constantly swinging a thick stick, the end of which burned slowly, to keep it aflame so that it could be used to light the firecrackers which were exploding every minute. When the first crackers went off like rifle-shots, the buzzards got frightened and left our procession to hide in the depths of the bush. But now they were accustomed to the noise and they

194

went with us all the way. Nobody throws stones at buzzards here or hurts them intentionally. The law protects the birds. But even if there were no law for the preservation of buzzards, the people would protect them, for they know them to be their health department, which disposes of carcasses.

Manuel marched all by himself as if he did not belong to this procession. Twice I went up to him and talked about Texas and about his job there. He answered and even tried to force a smile. When I saw how it pained him to talk, I left him alone for the rest of the way.

Old man Garcia stopped every once in a while, dragged the bottle out of his hip pocket, and took a shot. Both his friends who were helping him reach the cemetery on his own feet also helped him finish the bottle. Now and then another of his friends came up and was served. Garcia could afford to be generous, for should this bottle give out, he carried a second one in another pocket.

The mother walked in the midst of the crowd. Seeing her now, one would not believe her to be the principal mourner. No longer did she hang on the pump-master woman's arm for support. The heat and the rough trail would not allow it. The pump-master woman, however, still walked by her side, and a few other women were marching close by so that the mother could never feel alone, not even for a moment. They all chatted to shorten the trip and to forget the blazing·sun. They were talking of a thousand different things, but not of the kid. They were walking back to ordinary daily life.

The youngsters started to fight about whose turn it now was to carry the coffin. None of the boys wanted the honor, which before had been much coveted. The stench near the coffin had become unbearable even for the toughest of them. All had their handkerchiefs tied over their mouths and noses to protect them as much as possible from the horrible odor emanating from the box.

It was certainly a marvel how bravely the Garcia marched among the crowd, considering that she had not closed an eye during the past thirty-six hours, that she had received the most cruel beating from fate that any mother on earth could suffer, that for twenty hours she had wept, yelled, and lamented as never before in her life, and that she had eaten nothing since late afternoon the day before. Hers is a race which has a great future, provided it is not taken in by installment plans for buying things they can do without.

And there was another marvel, the musicians. The whole night through they had played dances, one right after the other without any intermission. If Indians dance, then they dance—there's no sitting out, and no gazing at the moon, either. They have time enough for staring at the moon when there is no music around.

Looking objectively at this show, I almost wondered whether anybody still considered it a funeral train. All were marching to the cemetery, no doubt, yet somehow it appeared as if the dead one had been dismissed long ago and the march now received its meaning solely from the music which was played. In spite of all my silent protests and solemn curses, American dances and torch songs had won after all, dominating all the senses and feelings of the marchers, who apparently preferred this music to that of their own land. My noble thoughts had made me but a preacher in the desert and I was positive that if I were to yell my disapproval of our night-club achievements, they would have believed me crazy from the scorching heat.

Perhaps they were right after all. Why should anybody have thought of death and of funerals? The world around us was green and full of life. The sky was blue, the sun golden. Butterflies by the thousands, some as big as two hands and others prettier than precious jewels, fluttered against the dark walls of the bush. Birds hidden in the thicket twittered noisily.

The jungle fiddled, sang, chirped so intensely that for seconds the music was drowned. Life was all around and everywhere and we maintained the silly notion that we were on a funeral march. Why didn't we leave that kid in the river, forget him, and have done with it? Why all the fuss? Wasn't he better off in the river than in a hole in the cemetery where dogs and hogs would dig him out and eat what was left of him? God gave him the river to play with, so we should have let him stay there and allowed him to be happy in his own way. Why did we interfere with the burial the Lord had prepared for him? Of course, since we had learned to be Christians we could no longer act like heathen and we had to do what was considered our Christian duty.

What the hell, if I only could concentrate on the march and not let my mind wander off all the time—and that's the reason why now I was stuck in a swampy hole and everybody was laughing at me! I wanted to be decent too; that's why I was marching and tripping over roots for a silly idea.

Long live the world which is so very funny to live in! What meaning to the living world had that little box of decomposing flesh? None. How insignificant is man in the universe, how insignificant his worries, his wars, his struggles, his ambitions, his trying to outwit his competitors! What is left of the great Cæsar? There would be one Rome just the same, Cæsar or no Cæsar. Perhaps it would not be on the river Tiber, but there would be one Rome. What will be left tomorrow of the dozen little Cæsars of today who think that they can build up a new world and terrify mankind? What are all the wars and dictatorships and bolshevisms for if finally men always end up by doing what is best for them, great men or not? So then why not enjoy life, love, merriment? And if some day you cannot enjoy them any longer, die and be forgotten and leave no ghosts behind. That's paradise.

33

 There, at last, the village was in sight. Huts, palm huts, grass huts, and one rotten imitation of an American bungalow. A multitude of naked children were running about. Chickens, hogs, turkeys, mules, goats, dogs in front of the huts, between them, inside them.

The people came out of their huts and in deep silence awaited the procession. And in deep silence they let it pass them. The men took off their hats as soon as the first mourners came near. Even the naked children stopped their playing and yelling and stared at us with wide-open eyes. A woman holding a baby in her arms shrieked when the marchers passed. Another woman looked around with harassed eyes, grasped her child playing at her feet, lifted him up, and folded her arms around him as if he were to be taken away from her. Then she cried out plaintively, and many of the women marching, among them the Garcia, joined her and howled in the same manner, as if they were answering calls of their kind.

Out of the general store a man staggered. He was dressed in a cheap white cotton suit, with a coat on, which is something I

198

had not seen for weeks. In his right hand he held a twig which he swished aimlessly through the air. He could hardly keep on his feet.

He was the teacher in the next village. Only for two months would he be in that village school, because the government paid that village only two months' salary for a teacher—a salary of seventy-five centavos a day. More than two months' salary the government could not spend on that Indian village. When the job was over, the teacher would return to town, where his family lived, and he would wait there for another assignment, which might come soon, which might come late, which might come never. It all depended on the teacher's personal friends and on their good standing with a diputado or another politician. Usually the teacher had to get the money for his return ticket by going from hut to hut and asking for as much as the parents of his pupils could spare; and as they were all very poor Indian peasants, it was not very much. After he had paid for his simple board and lodging in the village and sent the rest home to his wife and children, nothing of his salary was left for the ticket. But as a government employee he was entitled to a reduction of fifty per cent on a railroad ticket used in his capacity as a returning or outgoing teacher. This treatment of the teacher was caused not so much by a faulty government as by the fact that the resources of the republic are very limited and, as often happens in richer countries also, expenses for education and for schools in general come last. Soldiers always first. Another reason is that, just as elsewhere, politicians take twenty times more from the nation's income than is their legal share.

The school he taught in was a large room in a palm hut. No chair, no bench, no table could be found in the class-room. The children squatted on the earthen floor and put the paper on which they wrote upon their knees. Only the teacher had a crudely made chair, and a box for a table.

I had known the teacher when he taught in an Indian village about a hundred and twenty miles from here. I had been living there for a few months, and as I had had plenty of time, I had accompanied him on his Saturday excursions with the children to teach them the elements of geography, botany, insect life. In that village he had opened a night school for adults, since in the whole village there had been only five or six persons who could write and read, and no more than a dozen who could write their names.

Each grown-up pupil had paid him one peso a month, which considerably bettered his small income. I had visited this night school chiefly to get acquainted with my fellow students, to make friends with them and be welcome in their homes. This had been worth more to me than learning how to write my name without a mistake and learning whether the Spanish word for work is spelled with a v or a b. I had known ever since that he was a good teacher and that he deserved a better lot than being chased around from village to village.

That he had got pupils for his night school had not been due to the ambition of the people in the village, but to communist agitators who twice every month visited that village and told the young men that if they did not learn how to read and write they would never amount to anything and would be exploited by American imperialistic companies and by Spanish hacendados and German coffee-planters, and if they did not learn quickly, the United States would come and take the whole republic away from them and teach them the English language by force. The fact was that, because of the constant preaching of the communist agraristas, practically every young Indian had gone to night school and many of them had learned reading and writing fairly well in four months.

Seeing that teacher now, one might think him a common drunkard. I knew that he was as sober a man as any teacher anywhere. He was not Indian, more likely of Spanish descent with a heavy dash of Arabian blood. That he was drunk today was something which a hilarious fate had obviously prepared in advance. I knew something was going to take a different turn from what was expected. I only wondered what it would be and how it would come out. Fate was at play, or the teacher would not have been drunk.

Friends of the Garcia family who lived in that village had begged the teacher to come and say a few words over the kid's grave. The teacher knew the kid because the kid had gone to his school for a week when his father had had a job with the railroad. The job had lasted only a week, but during that week the kid's mother had sent him to the school near by, where the kid had learned to say: "An I which has no dot over it is no I."

The teacher had accepted the invitation to speak at the grave and had come to the village where the cemetery was. Here he had met the fathers of his pupils. On arriving, and not knowing any other place to go, he had stepped into the general store, where he had asked for a soda. In had come a man who was the father of two of his pupils. The father greeted the teacher and invited him to drink with him just one little copita of mescal. Beer was too expensive, and since there was no ice to be had, the beer was warm and therefore had no taste. To say no to such a kind invitation would have made the father believe that the teacher was too haughty to drink with an Indian. The teacher had a good heart. He knew how the father would feel if he were to refuse to drink with him. Even a soda or an orange crush costs more than a copita. So the teacher had drunk the hard mescal. The father of another pupil had then come in, and since he had accepted a drink from the first father, he could not refuse a drink from the second. Another father who had heard that the teacher was in the village stepped in and another drink was knocked down. Never more than just one little copita of mescal. But no matter how you

201

count, a certain number of copitas make a pint. The heat did the rest. God in heaven, how drunk that teacher was!

The procession marched on. Many of the villagers joined the mourners and went along with them. Far behind the rest the teacher was staggering along. He needed the whole road for himself. On his left arm hung that friend of Garcia who had invited the teacher to speak at the grave. This man was even more loaded than the teacher, whose knees might be weak, but some of whose senses were intact. But to drag along a drunken companion who did not make the slightest effort to keep on his own feet—that, surely, was a dangerous task for one who had to fight hard himself against those spirits which are so very friendly to man the first three times, but are nasty fellows after the tenth.

The teacher tried his best to show that he was a dignified personage. His companion, however, walking practically upon his knees, dragged and pulled the poor teacher every few paces down to the ground. That drunken friend stumbled and tripped and fell, and the good-natured teacher had to lift him up again to his feet. That job made the teacher seem more drunk than he actually was at the time the mourners arrived at the village.

34

 The procession reached the cemetery. What a
cemetery! It was one more proof of the fact that
Christianity had not yet come to the Indians, but instead a
degenerated, corrupted religion dolled up with empty cere-
monies borrowed from the Roman Catholicism of the first half
of the sixteenth century.

The gate consisted of two lattice wings made of sticks. The
gate was purely for decorative purposes because one could
enter the place at either side of the gate, where the fence had
rotted and collapsed; from the posts hung rusty barbed wire,
some of which was lying on the ground.

From the top of the center gate post a cross greeted the
visitor. Three little hillocks covered with withered flowers and
simple crosses without names on them were the only signs that
this place was supposed to be a cemetery. Everything else
looked like what the earth will look like on doomsday late in
the afternoon.

There were a great number of little mounds. None had the
shape of a grave. All these mounds were overgrown with wiry

grass and thorny bushes which had been trampled upon, and most of the mounds had been dug open, obviously by dogs, hogs, and wild beasts searching the ground for tasty morsels. Bones were strewn all over the place, but mercifully hidden by the high grass. Rotten boards from decayed coffins were lying everywhere. A score of crude crosses were lying flat on the ground. And this ground was richly decorated with the dung of cows, horses, burros, mules, and dogs wherever you looked or walked. The funny thing about that cemetery was that I liked it immensely. If I cannot be dropped into the sea, which by all means I prefer, I should like to be buried silently in a cemetery of that kind, and, please, send no flowers.

We make too much fuss over our dead. We believe them holy or saintly and treat them accordingly. A dead one is dead. He has left us and we ought to leave him in peace. He should be forgotten the moment he is covered with earth or sent up in smoke. The billions we spend on our dead would serve mankind better if they were spent on more hospitals, on prepaid doctors' fees, and on more research on disease. It would be more human and surely more civilized if instead of wasting billions upon the dead we spent that money on the living to keep them sane and healthy and so have them longer with us. Just on the flowers that are thrown to the dead, who cannot see or smell them, we could save enough money to take care of ten thousand babies every year and make their mothers happy.

I wondered if that teacher and his companion would ever reach the cemetery. Now he was floored, now the other was.

At last we were standing before the open grave. There were no grave-diggers about. The grave had to be dug by the father or a relative or a neighbor. In this case Manuel had dug the hole. He had done the job early in the morning when it was cool. Then he had hurried back on horseback to be ready to follow the procession.

The coffin was put on the ground a few feet away from the

hole. The coffin-maker pulled out the two nails and took off the lid so that the mother could see her baby for the last time. It was also the law, which ordered that a coffin must be opened just before it is let down so that the mourners may convince themselves they have the right corpse and are not by mistake burying the wrong one. It was furthermore the last chance for the dead to come back to life if he thought he was not yet fully dead and could afford to hang on a while longer. With the coffin open, practically nothing of the body was visible. The box was apparently filled only with a mass of colored paper, a golden crown, and a scepter from which the paper was already peeling off. The face was covered by the crown, which had dropped over it and hid its ghastly ugliness. The bared teeth grinning out from under the crown were the only evidence that the crumbling mass of wet colored paper hid the remains of a human body.

With a terrific outcry the Garcia threw herself across the open coffin and embraced the whole box. Her crying ebbed to a long, bitter whimpering.

And while her body shook violently from inner convulsions, the little wooden whistle, which she had caught when it had fallen out of the kid's pants' pocket after he had been fished out of the river, dropped at this moment out of the bosom of her dress. The whistle fell on the ground. She stared at it, ceased whimpering immediately, picked up the whistle, pressed it against her lips, and quickly, as if she might forget it, she hid it inside the paper frocks and said in a low voice: "Here, mi nene, chiquito mio, don't leave your whistle behind. And forgive me, chiquitito mio, my beloved darling, that I spanked you because you wouldn't stop blowing that whistle all the time right into my ears, and that made me so very angry. You forgive me, won't you, Carlitos mio?"

All the women, on hearing her speak to her baby as if he could still hear her, started sobbing.

205

Garcia, half staggering, half stumbling, came up to the grave. He leaned against the two men who had supported him. He could no longer stand up by himself, because his second bottle, which he had kept in reserve, had in the meantime been finished.

He considered it his right to stand before all the other people beside the open box, for he was the father, drunk or not. He opened his mouth to say something to the crowd. Perhaps he wished to cry, but only a little squeak came out. With one hand he wiped off the thick tears which were rolling down his cheeks. In spite of his drunkenness and all the numbness in his head, he realized fully that his little boy was leaving him forever.

All the women were weeping bitterly as if the child were their own. The pump-master woman, assisted by another woman, went close to the box and lifted the Garcia up from the ground on which she had fallen exhausted.

No sooner did the coffin-maker see the box freed from the mother's attention than he put the lid on, and in a few seconds it was nailed fast—this time for good.

Then it was carried to the hole.

35

　　Now everybody turns his head around towards the gate and waits for the teacher to appear. He is still outside. Ashamed to meet the weeping mother and the crowd of mourners in his present condition, he refuses to enter the grounds. But his companion finally pushes him through the gate. When the teacher still resists going farther, that fellow, despite his being so drunk, has sense enough to wink to another man, who immediately approaches and leads the teacher to the grave.

After much labor and time the teacher is at last standing at the edge of the open hole. All look at him in anticipation of his speech.

Swaying dangerously, he stares at the mother. His eyes get moist and with an energetic twist he turns around and runs away. His companion, the friend of the Garcias, wakens from his torpidity just long enough to note the teacher's retreat and he yells after him to come back immediately and keep his promise like a real he-man and look the goddamned world bravely in the face. As the teacher does not heed his yells, he starts to swear terribly, until he is stopped by two men who slap him straight upon his hatchway, which censure astonishes him so much that he forgets what he was doing and why he was yelling.

A few other drunks take up the call and holler to the teacher not to be a deserter of the poor and ignorant. Sober men try to quiet the unruly shouters, telling them to pardon the teacher, as they could see what a state he is in. This fails entirely, and one of the drunken callers, just to show the crowd that nobody on earth, not even that goddamned son of an old hussy—the president of the whole damned republic—can tell him what to do, he now roars like an angered bull and insults the teacher in the most filthy manner.

Well, it is about to become a lively funeral after all.

The sober men, seeing no other way to calm the drunks, and too decent to give them a well-deserved thrashing right here in the graveyard, go after the teacher and beg him, please, to come back and just say a few little palabras, muy pocas palabras, which will do all right, and never mind the condition he is in, because everybody understands that and all of us are human and nobody thinks himself fit to blame or reproach his fellow men.

The teacher cannot answer audibly. He only jabbers incoherently. Turning around, he struggles clumsily to free himself from those who want to bring him back. While still struggling, he suddenly sees the weeping mother, who silently and tearfully looks straight into his eyes. He immediately stops his struggle and stares at the mother as if he were awakening from a dream. Perhaps just because his brain is befogged, he detects something in the stare of the mother which others cannot see. For a few seconds he stands still as if listening to something which speaks to him from the inside, while his eyes are firmly fixed upon the mother's face. Then he goes slowly to the grave.

Once more he stands in front of the hole, his body swaying in every direction. Both his arms gesticulate for a while before he opens his lips. Still holding the twig in his right hand, he looks savagely around as if he were going to fight an invisible enemy who is defending himself with a sword. His dull and glassy eyes gaze into emptiness. The hundred or more faces before him must surely be making a horrible impression upon his numb mind. He apparently sees in this lake of faces a monster creeping towards him, because his features are distorted with terror.

It cannot be stage fright, for I have heard him speak on a national holiday, and from that occasion I know that he is a fairly good orator who is not afraid of speaking before a crowd.

And now all of a sudden he throws both his arms up, opens his mouth, and then closes it almost automatically. This he does several times. It seems he thinks that he is speaking, yet not one word can be heard.

Now he shouts with great force: "We all assembled here are very sad. Very, very sad indeed, that's what we are, all of us who are gathered here, God and men know why and what for."

These words he shouts so loudly that if there were six thousand people present, all scattered over a wide plain, they could be heard by everybody.

Again he yells, and this time as if speaking to twenty thousand: "The little boy is dead. He is completely dead. I am sure of that. We'll never see him again. We shall never, as long as this world may exist, never more hear his innocent and happy laughter."

Tears swell in his eyes.

All this was nothing. He now lifts his voice as if he had a good mind to split open the skies: "The mother of that little boy of ours is very sad too. Yes, you folks, believe me, she is very sad, because she is the mother and she no longer has her baby with her to play with."

He looks over all the people without seeing one in particular and he yells: "I tell you, folks, the mother is grief-stricken. She weeps. You can see that for yourself. She has been weeping all through this terrible night, the mother has, and you people, you have to believe me." While thus shouting, he grasps his twig firmly and whips it through the air with all his might as if he meant to slay anyone who dared doubt that the mother is very sad and that she weeps for her baby.

That stroke at his invisible enemy, whom he apparently considers the mother's enemy also, was well meant and it surely was an honest stroke. But it was too much for his wavering body. He tumbles over, straight into the hole in front of him. He does not quite reach the bottom, though, thanks to the two poles laid across the hole on which the coffin should be standing. Fortunately for him, it had not yet been put there. Owing to the long fight to get the teacher back to the grave, this part of the ceremony had been overlooked and the box is still on the opposite edge of the hole.

The teacher had grasped one of these poles and now is hanging from it helplessly. With his legs he struggles ridiculously to reach the edge and climb out. His fight proves vain, and if at this precious moment brotherly assistance had not come to his rescue, he would have fallen down to the bottom, from which he could never have got out until the next morning.

And now a very strange thing happens.

The fall of the respectable teacher, his pitiful and clumsy struggle to get out again, his hanging on that pole like an old, lame monkey—all happening at such a moment—makes the funniest show I can imagine. But not a single person, man, woman, girl, or boy, laughs at the teacher. I, for one, usually have great difficulty keeping from laughing. It has happened to

210

me more than once, that I have had to leave a church quickly to avoid a scandal, because practically every minister, with his pretended dignity and his silly sermons, makes me giggle and after a while break out into open laughter. I cannot help it that I see most things in a funny way, and if I fail to see fun in supposedly sacred performances or speeches, then I can see only the irony in them. And yet here I do not laugh; even were I tickled I would not have laughed, for I can see neither fun nor irony in the situation. Instead, it makes me cry for the first time since the kid was fished out of the river. Years have passed since those twenty-two hours when the Great Bandmaster was down on earth to play the music for one of the wildest and hottest dances I have ever seen. And still to this day I cannot laugh at this apparently funny situation. No one laughed. I know today as I knew then why no man laughed. Nobody laughed; neither did I, because I was one of them, and it was my boy who was to be buried just as he was the child of everybody present. No teacher was struggling to come out of a grave into which he had fallen. I saw only a great brotherly love for his fellow men which had dropped into the grave and was struggling so hard to get out again. I can laugh at a thousand things and situations—even at the brutalities of fascism, which as I see them are but a ridiculous cowardice without limits. But I can never laugh at love shown by men for those of their fellow men in pain and sorrow. This love I witnessed was coming straight from the heart; it was honest and true as only love can be for which no one expects thanks because every one of us gathered here, not excluding the teacher, had lost a beloved baby.

And the teacher once more stands at the grave, the twig still in his right hand. Even while he struggled he had not let go of his twig, which seems to be the staff on which he leans for his safety in a cruel world.

He stands there looking as if all that had just happened had nothing to do with him, but had happened to somebody else whom he does not know, and he stands there as if he were waiting for the disturbance to cease so that he can go on with his speech.

Yelling much louder than before, he says: "The father who is with us on this unlucky day is also very, very sad. Yes, my friends, believe me, the father is very sad and he weeps as does the mother. You have to believe that, folks."

Again his twig slashes the air. But this time he has taken better care of himself. He stays about three feet away from the grave, far enough so that if he should trip again, he would not fall in. Besides, this time he does not whip forward. He has learned from his first mistake. This time he whips along his right side as if he were sitting on a horse. So he does not fall towards the grave, but merely whirls around a few times. Then he gets set firmly on the ground again.

He faces the crowd. Nobody laughs.

"The little boy had to die so soon," he yells, and whips the air. "The good little boy had to die so very soon, and he is dead. We have all loved him very much. We have been happy when he was with us. Now he is gone. For this we feel very sorry and blame none. It had to be. He is dead. Now we will bury him. Adiós, my little boy, adiosito!"

Would that the buzzards had taken the whole funeral somewhere else. I weep and howl like the old watchdog of a haunted castle in Scotland at midnight when visited by the ghost of an old duchess who had been changed into a rattling lamppost. I weep and howl and the whole crowd weeps and howls; the whole crowd, men, women, children, and even the crumbs of the dry soil shed tears and blubber. It is no longer the shrieking of the night. It is a mournful weeping as if it were over something which had happened centuries ago and was now recalled to mind by a well-written narrative.

What do I care about that kid? An Indian boy whom I

hardly noticed, whom I have known only for a few hours. None the less I weep over him. Perhaps he is my own boy after all, my boy as well as the boy of all the others here, my boy as well as the boy of every mother everywhere on earth. Why should he be somebody else's boy? He is my boy, my little brother, my fellow man, who could suffer as I can, who could laugh as I can, and who could die as I shall die some day.

36

 Two men try to lower the coffin with lassos, but the poles on which they are standing shake, wobble, and roll over and there is some difficulty getting the lassos straight.

On seeing this confusion a man jumped into the grave.

"Give me that box," he says in a businesslike manner to those standing above.

The man climbs up again.

Mother and father are throwing handfuls of earth into the grave.

Manuel then does the same, but he has very little soil in his hands.

And now earth is thrown in from all sides and from every hand.

The musicians step up to the spot where shortly before the teacher had made his speech. Surely they will now play *Ave Maria* or *Nearer, My God, to Thee*, or something like that. I am honestly afraid that they will commit such a sin. After all, they are only Christians and are supposed to do what is considered right and decent.

214

God Almighty, I thank You, because I feel relieved of a pain. The musicians have excellent taste. I knew I could trust them. They know how to press the right button at the right time. They are not hypocrites and they will do nothing which does not come out of their sane hearts. True children of the jungle, they call everything by its right name and give back to nature what belongs to nature.

And so these admirable men are playing once more the great, immortal funeral march of mankind, *Taintgonna*. I frankly admit that I could embrace them.

While they are playing the song of songs with enthusiasm and fervor, youngsters are shoveling earth into the grave. Women arrange the flowers and wreaths. The mother, softly weeping, is surrounded by a crowd of women who, one after the other, embrace and kiss her while telling her how dearly loved she is by everybody. The men cover their heads, roll cigarettes, and wait patiently. No one leaves the graveyard until the mother gives permission to do so by leaving first.

What to do now? Something should be done while everybody waits.

The musicians, having finished their piece, are waiting too. As the pause lasts longer than they expected, they think it would be highly appreciated by all if they played another piece until the grave is covered, the flowers all placed on it, and the mother ready to leave. So they remember the other funeral march, that of about sixteen years or so back, which was produced by exactly the same brain disease as was the first.

Well now, let me see, isn't that the beautiful song which was invented soon after the day when soldiers home from France tried to collect on that wonderful promise: "Your country will never forget you! Others have joined, why not U! Do it now! Your country will never never—"? So help me God, how could I forget? Because it *is* the song all right, the song which kept in check the angry fist which was threatening to do some face-lifting on the old world. It is the song all right. It came then at the proper time as it comes now to this Indian country. *Yeswehavenobananastoday.* Yea, my good man, yes, I cannot give you a job today, or food, or a coat, or anything at all; but you see I can sing you a song which will fill your belly with beans of lead should you ever try to eat without having a job. Yes, of course, we have nobananas.

Adiós, my beloved little boy! Adiós! Worms and maggots are going to live and fatten. But you, my little boy, you had to die. Adiós! No king was ever buried the way you were. Adiosito!

FOR thirty-five years, from 1876 to 1911, power in Mexico was in the hands of one man, Porfirio Díaz. Mexico's constitution had been altered to sanction his reelections, which were assured by his appointment of state governors and other officials. Opposition was controlled by a ruthless federal police called the *rurales*. It was a reign of peace and prosperity for the few and dire poverty for the many—half the entire rural population of Mexico was bound to debt slavery. Big landowners and foreign capital were favored as more and more Indians lost their communal lands.

In the final decade of Díaz's rule, however, opposition strengthened, and before his last engineered reelection he promised a return to democratic forms—which after the election he gave no signs of honoring. In 1910 revolution broke out; independent rebel armies under the leadership of Pancho Villa, Emiliano Zapata, Francisco Madero, and others upset the power of the landlords and eventually overthrew the Díaz regime.

In what have become known as the "Jungle Novels," B. Traven wrote during the 1930s an epic of the birth of the Mexican revolution. The six novels—*Government, The Carreta, March to the Montería, Trozas, The Rebellion of the Hanged,* and *The General from the Jungle*—describe the conditions of peonage and debt slavery under which the Indians suffered in Díaz's time. The novels follow the spirit of rebellion that slowly spread through the labor camps and haciendas, culminating in the bloody revolt that ended Porfirio Díaz's rule.

In the 1920s, when B. Traven arrived in the country, peonage, although officially abolished by the new constitution of 1917, was still a general practice in many parts of Mexico. The author observed the system firsthand in Chiapas, the southernmost province, a mountainous and heavily forested region where the Jungle Novels, as well as many other of his stories, are set.

The mysterious B. Traven (1890–1969) was born in Chicago, spent his youth in Germany as an itinerant actor and revolutionary journalist, became a seaman on tramp steamers, settled in Mexico in the early 1920s, and began recording his experiences in novels and stories.

Ivan R. Dee is republishing eight novels and books of short stories by B. Traven, and is publishing the first translation into English of *Trozas*, the fourth of the Jungle Novels.

ELEPHANT PAPERBACKS

Literature and Letters
Stephen Vincent Benét, *John Brown's Body*, EL10
Isaiah Berlin, *The Hedgehog and the Fox*, EL21
Anthony Burgess, *Shakespeare*, EL27
Philip Callow, *Son and Lover: The Young D. H. Lawrence*, EL14
James Gould Cozzens, *Castaway*, EL6
James Gould Cozzens, *Men and Brethren*, EL3
Clarence Darrow, *Verdicts Out of Court*, EL2
Floyd Dell, *Intellectual Vagabondage*, EL13
Theodore Dreiser, *Best Short Stories*, EL1
Joseph Epstein, *Ambition*, EL7
André Gide, *Madeleine*, EL8
John Gross, *The Rise and Fall of the Man of Letters*, EL18
Irving Howe, *William Faulkner*, EL15
Aldous Huxley, *After Many a Summer Dies the Swan*, EL20
Aldous Huxley, *Ape and Essence*, EL19
Aldous Huxley, *Collected Short Stories*, EL17
Sinclair Lewis, *Selected Short Stories*, EL9
William L. O'Neill, ed., *Echoes of Revolt: The Masses,
    1911–1917*, EL5
Ramón J. Sender, *Seven Red Sundays*, EL11
Wilfrid Sheed, *Office Politics*, EL4
Tess Slesinger, *On Being Told That Her Second Husband Has
    Taken His First Lover, and Other Stories*, EL12
B. Traven, *The Bridge in the Jungle*, EL28
B. Traven, *The Carreta*, EL25
B. Traven, *Government*, EL23
B. Traven, *March to the Montería*, EL26
B. Traven, *The Night Visitor and Other Stories*, EL24
B. Traven, *The Rebellion of the Hanged*, EL29
Rex Warner, *The Aerodrome*, EL22
Thomas Wolfe, *The Hills Beyond*, EL16

Theatre and Drama
Robert Brustein, *Reimagining American Theatre*, EL410
Robert Brustein, *The Theatre of Revolt*, EL407
Irina and Igor Levin, *Working on the Play and the Role*, EL411
Plays for Performance:
    Aristophanes, *Lysistrata*, EL405
    Pierre Augustin de Beaumarchais, *The Marriage of Figaro*,
        EL418
    Anton Chekhov, *The Seagull*, EL407
    Fyodor Dostoevsky, *Crime and Punishment*, EL416
    Euripides, *The Bacchae*, EL419
    Georges Feydeau, *Paradise Hotel*, EL403
    Henrik Ibsen, *Ghosts*, EL401
    Henrik Ibsen, *Hedda Gabler*, EL413
    Henrik Ibsen, *The Master Builder*, EL417
    Henrik Ibsen, *When We Dead Awaken*, EL408
    Heinrich von Kleist, *The Prince of Homburg*, EL402
    Christopher Marlowe, *Doctor Faustus*, EL404
    The Mysteries: Creation, EL412
    The Mysteries: The Passion, EL414
    Sophocles, *Electra*, EL415
    August Strindberg, *The Father*, EL406

ELEPHANT PAPERBACKS

American History and American Studies
Stephen Vincent Benét, *John Brown's Body*, EL10
Henry W. Berger, ed., *A William Appleman Williams Reader*, EL126
Andrew Bergman, *We're in the Money*, EL124
Paul Boyer, ed., *Reagan as President*, EL117
Robert V. Bruce, *1877: Year of Violence*, EL102
George Dangerfield, *The Era of Good Feelings*, EL110
Clarence Darrow, *Verdicts Out of Court*, EL2
Floyd Dell, *Intellectual Vagabondage*, EL13
Elisha P. Douglass, *Rebels and Democrats*, EL108
Theodore Draper, *The Roots of American Communism*, EL105
Joseph Epstein, *Ambition*, EL7
Lloyd C. Gardner, *Spheres of Influence*, EL131
Paul W. Glad, *McKinley, Bryan, and the People*, EL119
Daniel Horowitz, *The Morality of Spending*, EL122
Kenneth T. Jackson, *The Ku Klux Klan in the City, 1915–1930*, EL123
Edward Chase Kirkland, *Dream and Thought in the Business Community, 1860–1900*, EL114
Herbert S Klein, *Slavery in the Americas*, EL103
Aileen S. Kraditor, *Means and Ends in American Abolitionism*, EL111
Leonard W. Levy, *Jefferson and Civil Liberties: The Darker Side*, EL107
Seymour J. Mandelbaum, *Boss Tweed's New York*, EL112
Thomas J. McCormick, *China Market*, EL115
Walter Millis, *The Martial Spirit*, EL104
Nicolaus Mills, ed., *Culture in an Age of Money*, EL302
Nicolaus Mills, *Like a Holy Crusade*, EL129
Roderick Nash, *The Nervous Generation*, EL113
William L. O'Neill, ed., *Echoes of Revolt: The Masses, 1911–1917*, EL5
Glenn Porter and Harold C. Livesay, *Merchants and Manufacturers*, EL106
Edward Reynolds, *Stand the Storm*, EL128
Geoffrey S. Smith, *To Save a Nation*, EL125
Bernard Sternsher, ed., *Hitting Home: The Great Depression in Town and Country*, EL109
Athan Theoharis, *From the Secret Files of J. Edgar Hoover*, EL127
Nicholas von Hoffman, *We Are the People Our Parents Warned Us Against*, EL301
Norman Ware, *The Industrial Worker, 1840–1860*, EL116
Tom Wicker, *JFK and LBJ: The Influence of Personality upon Politics*, EL120
Robert H. Wiebe, *Businessmen and Reform*, EL101
T. Harry Williams, *McClellan, Sherman and Grant*, EL121
Miles Wolff, *Lunch at the 5 & 10*, EL118
Randall B. Woods and Howard Jones, *Dawning of the Cold War*, EL130

European and World History
Mark Frankland, *The Patriots' Revolution*, EL201
Lloyd C. Gardner, *Spheres of Influence*, EL131
Thomas A. Idinopulos, *Jerusalem*, EL204
Ronnie S. Landau, *The Nazi Holocaust*, EL203
Clive Ponting, *1940: Myth and Reality*, EL202

CPSIA information can be obtained at www.ICGtesting.com
Printed in the USA
BVOW05s0243310815

415837BV00001B/11/P